THE ALMOST MEETING

Henry Kreisel

NeWest Press
Edmonton

Some of these stories were broadcast on the CBC and have appeared in the following journals: The Literary Review, Prism, Queen's Quarterly, and Tamarack Review.

Canadian Cataloguing in Publication Data

Kreisel, Henry, 1922-
        The almost meeting

        ISBN 0-912316-13-1
        I. Title.
        PS8521.R44A159 1981   C813'.54   C81-091091-8
        PR9199.3.K74A78

Published by NeWest Publishers Ltd., "The Western Publishers", 204-10711-107 Ave., Edmonton, Alberta   T6C 0W6.

Manufactured in Western Canada.

THE ALMOST MEETING

To Philip,
my son and my friend

Contents

The Almost Meeting

The Almost Meeting

The letter was addressed to Alexander Budak in care of his publisher in Toronto, and the publisher had sent it on to him in Edmonton, where he lived. Both the address and the note itself were hand-written, and Alexander Budak was at once struck by the unusual way in which the letters had been formed. The writer had used the thinnest possible nib, and his writing looked like an intricate web spun by a long-legged spider. At first Alexander Budak thought that it would be impossible for him to decipher the writing, but as he stared at it, he could make out a Toronto address and a date, and then he glanced down the page and saw the signature. "David Lasker." Alexander Budak was intrigued, even excited. For it was a legendary name. Many people regarded David Lasker as one of the greatest writers the country had produced, a great poet as well as a great novelist, who had created an astonishing body of work, but had then suddenly fallen silent. During the last ten years or so he had published virtually nothing. Only once, about two years ago, a new group of his poems had appeared in the *Canadian Forum*. They were enigmatic utterances, but full of the most striking images, in which the artist seemed to want to refine himself out of existence, to separate his fleshly self

11

from the works of his own creation until all that was bound up with the self was burned away. The poet himself would become a zero. Only the created work would glimmer and shine in its anonymity.

It was a far cry from the earlier Lasker, a flamboyant character who wore outrageous clothes and let his hair grow long when that was considered offensive, and who delighted to shock and scandalize the respectable middle class of Toronto and of English Canada in general, even the people (particularly the people) who rarely read his serious work, but knew of him only through the stories that appeared in the week-end supplements of the daily papers.

Lasker's writing had a voluptuous quality that Alexander Budak admired. It was full of passion and emotion. Lasker had given a voice to the immigrants who had come to Canada in the early years of the century. His first book of poems presented a marvellous gallery of the Jewish immigrants, the men and women of his parents' generation, but then he had gone beyond his own community and had written some wonderful things about the immigrants who had come to the city after the second world war — the Greeks and Italians and the people from Eastern Europe — and of their impact on what was still a staid and proper puritan city.

Often in his writing people of different nationalities came together and almost touched, only to find themselves pulled apart again. Alexander Budak was hoping that Lasker might have something to say about reconciliation between people, for he had a wonderful gift of moving easily between different ethnic groups and of comprehending and communicating nuances of feeling. But just when it seemed to Alexander Budak that Lasker might hold out the hope that solitudes could touch and intertwine, he had fallen silent, had drawn into himself, and apart from a few enigmatic utterances, had published nothing.

Nonetheless, his achievement stood. He had given voice to the voiceless, had made invisible men and women visible, and when Alexander Budak was driven to write himself, David Lasker's example was of prime importance. He took heart from him when he tried to set down the story that ultimately became his first novel. When he had doubts about what he was doing, he read Lasker, and that gave him courage to go on. His novel began by tracing the life of an immigrant who had come to Canada in the aftermath of the first world war from the border region of Croatia and Hungary. This man, to whom Alexander Budak gave the name of Lukas, had gone first to Ontario, and then had drifted West, worked on farms, and then came to Edmonton, where he found work in a scrap-yard.

There he met Helena, one of the girls who worked in the office, and fell in love with her. She was a vivacious girl who'd come to Canada with her parents when she was a baby. The family came from the same border region as Lukas, but they belonged to a different nationality, and they brought with them all the hostility and all the ancient enmities that were endemic in the border region.

Helena knew that the thought of her having any kind of relationship with Lukas would be unbearable to her parents, and for a long time she resisted his advances. But Lukas was strong and handsome, his eyes glowing like coals, his thick hair black and shiny. She could not resist him.

They began to have their lunch together, sandwiches they had brought from home. Occasionally he dared to take her hand. It was as if an electric current passed through her. Then one day he asked her to have lunch with him in a restaurant. It took her a week to make up her mind because she knew that if she accepted she would have consented to the start of a serious relationship. Although he had not told her, she knew that he was in love with her, and though she did not yet admit it to herself, she was already half in love with him. And so she finally agreed to that innocent lunch in a restaurant.

From then on things moved quickly. She fell passionately in love with him. She could not wait to go to work in the morning because she would see him and at lunch they would be together.

At home, the family noticed the change. One Sunday after they had all returned from mass, her father, his long mustaches bristling, said that she was love-sick. Demanded to know who the man was. She denied at first that there was any involvement with a man, but the family wore her down and she confessed that she was in love. With a man she had met at work. Who was he? they demanded to know. What was him name? Lukas, she whispered. A wonderful man, she said. What was his religion? He was a Catholic. Her mother crossed herself. A burden had been lifted. Thank God, he was not a Lutheran or a Jew.

Her father was not so quickly appeased. Where did he come from, this wonderful man? What wind had blown him here? She mumbled the name of a border town. Her voice was barely audible, but her father's hearing was as sharp as a fox's and he knew at once why she had kept the knowledge from them. He repeated the name of the town in a roaring voice that sounded and resounded through the house. They cowered away from him, the girl and her mother, and her brother and her sister.

No answer was necessary or indeed expected. The name of that town was alone sufficient to proclaim her transgression. How could she do such a thing? How could she bring shame on the family?

Her face became flushed, she felt her anger rising, her hands began to tremble. For the first time in her life she found herself in open rebellion against her father. She had always loved him and had, according to the tradition of her family, obeyed him. But now he suddenly appeared to her as a tyrannous, vindictive man. She was shocked by her own feeling, but she could not suppress it.

This was Canada, she said in a soft voice, and she was an adult now.

He snorted his contempt. She lived in his house, he snarled, she was his daughter, and she would obey. The honour of the whole family was involved.

This reasoning, which only a few weeks ago she would have unquestioningly accepted, now seemed to her absurd. She was defiant. She refused to bend the knee. Instead, she got her coat and rushed out of the house.

She knew the house where Lukas rented a room. He was astonished when she appeared at his door, on a Sunday, in the middle of the day. Under the disapproving eye of his landlady, she slipped into his room. She was agitated and excited. Lukas had never seen her look so beautiful. He took her in his arms and she told her story.

What was she going to do? he asked. It was not what *she* was going to do, she answered without any hesitation, for she had already made the decision, it was what *they* were going to do. They must get married, she said. At once. She was her father's daughter after all, she had his determination and power.

Lukas was quite overwhelmed. He was also afraid. How would they manage? She was not afraid. She felt free, as if shackles had been removed from her wrists. Her heady feeling, her exhilaration was infectious. With a cry he grasped her in his arms and pulled her down onto his bed and kissed her passionately. She did not lose control. She allowed him to touch her breasts and the inside of her thighs, and she responded passionately to his kisses. But then she freed herself from his embrace and said, not yet, not here.

She spent the night in a hotel, alone, and the next day found herself a room and moved out of her father's house. Soon afterwards, they were married, Lukas and she, with only the officiating priest there, and two of their co-workers as witnesses.

Her father disowned her publicly. He would have nothing to do with her, and he forbade her mother to get in touch with her, though occasionally they made contact, but only fleetingly.

Not even the birth of their first child, a girl, changed

things. She ached to show the child to her parents, but her father's door remained closed. Once, on a Saturday in the farmers' market on 97th Street, she was wheeling the baby in her carriage, and she saw her mother from afar and her mother saw her. Her mother remained rooted to the spot where she stood and Helena slowly moved towards her. Her mother looked oh so longingly at the baby in the carriage and tears were coursing down her cheeks, but she made no sound, and then Helena saw her father some ten or twelve feet away at a stall where he had just bought potatoes. He looked away sternly — she could see that he was trembling, that it took a superhuman effort for him not to look at his granddaughter — but he would not do it.

It was the most shattering experience Helena had ever had. When she got home she broke down and could not control her sobbing and crying, and it was a long time before she could tell the uncomprehending Lukas what had happened to her.

A few days later she found that she was pregnant again. It was almost more than she could bear, but then the thought came to her that if the new child was a boy, her father would relent. He would not be able to keep away from a grandson.

She gave birth to a son and she was jubilant. But the change she had hoped for did not occur. Her father did not relent. His door remained closed.

In her rage Helena turned against her husband. She blamed Lukas for her despair. The marriage could not stand the strain. Lukas did not know how to handle an emotional situation he could barely comprehend.

One day he did not return from work. He disappeared. No one knew where he had gone. The earth had swallowed him up.

She was deserted and alone and desperate. And only then did her father open his door to her. He had said that nothing good could come of the marriage and now he had been proved right. Now he could take possession of his grandchildren and bring them up and enjoy them. But Helena was defeated and in

16

a sense she never recovered.

The little boy loved his grandfather, and it was not until he was fourteen or fifteen that he began to understand what had happened. His mother told him the story over and over again. His grandfather had robbed him of his father and he had robbed her of her husband. The boy's love for his grandfather turned to something akin to hate. When he was just over fourteen, the boy ran away from his grandfather's house to find his father. He did not know where to begin. After two days the police picked him up and took him back home, and his grandfather punished him. But now his mind was made up and his mother encouraged him because this was a way in which she could have her revenge against her father.

When the boy was seventeen he left his grandfather's house for good and set out to find his father. It was a quest that was to take him across Canada and into the United States. He picked up the trail of his father, and his search took him north to Yellowknife, and then to the East coast and to the West coast, and into California. Twice he almost found Lukas, only to have him vanish before he could meet him face to face.

That was the story Alexander Budak told in his first novel. It was his own story and the story of his family, and he told it with honesty and great power. It had created a stir. And now David Lasker had written to him.

The letter, written in that strange hand-writing that looked like the intricate web spun by a long-legged spider, was brief.

"I salute you," Lasker had written. "How sad. How sad. How we torture each other. I sense a bitterness in your hero because he cannot find his father. Let him not despair. An almost meeting is often more important than the meeting. The quest is all."

What did that mean? Alexander Budak sat down at once to answer Lasker. "You have meant much to me," he wrote. "Without your example I could never have become a writer. You gave me courage to write my novel. I'm going to be in

17

Toronto in December and want very much to see you. I have much to ask you."

Three weeks later Alexander Budak received another letter from Lasker. It contained only one word. "Perhaps."

When Alexander Budak came to Toronto in December, sent there by his publisher to promote his novel, snow was already on the ground. His letter to Lasker, telling him when he was coming, had gone unanswered. And when he checked the Toronto telephone directory, Lasker's number was not listed. So it appeared to Alexander Budak that he would not be able to meet Lasker after all.

On the second evening of his stay in Toronto, Alexander Budak had dinner at the apartment of Robert Walker, a writer of Lasker's generation, and once one of his closest friends. Alexander Budak told him of the exchange of letters he'd had with Lasker. He wanted desperately to see him, he said.

"That might be difficult," said Walker. "He doesn't see many people any more."

"Why?" asked Alexander Budak.

"I wish I knew. I could spin some theories, but they wouldn't explain anything. Perhaps he's himself said all that can be said in his last poems. Perhaps the human condition has become too much for him to bear." He thought for a while. Then he said, "I haven't seen him for two or three years. But I still have his telephone number. Why don't I phone him? Perhaps he'll see you, since he's obviously interested in your work."

He left the dining-room to phone and after a few minutes returned. "He wouldn't come to the phone himself," he said. "But I spoke to his wife and she acted as go-between. It was a strange sensation, since he must have been right there. She said he was excited to hear that you were in town. Believe it or not, he said he wants to meet you and he's going to come here. It'll take him a half hour or so. I'm amazed. I didn't think he would actually agree to come."

They waited, drinking their after-dinner coffee.

Alexander Budak felt a growing sense of excitement, as if he expected from Lasker some kind of revelation.

The phone rang and Walker went to answer it. When he came back into the dining-room, he looked puzzled.

"This was the strangest call," he said. "It was the man who runs a little grocery store a couple of blocks from here. He said a gentleman was in the store and would like me to come and get him. 'Who is he?' I asked. 'Can I speak to him?' The grocer said, 'That's what I wanted him to do, but he said he didn't want to talk on the phone. He wants you to come down here and fetch him. He says he might get lost.' 'Is his name Lasker?' I asked. 'I'll ask him,' said the grocer, and after a moment he said to me, 'The gentleman says he might be. He says it's possible.' Then he whispered into the phone, 'It's weird. You better get here.' "

Walker looked at Alexander Budak. "I'm worried," he said. "Let's hurry down. He may not be well. He may need help."

The snow was coming down hard and it made walking difficult. It took them more than five minutes to walk the two blocks to the grocery store. A little bell tinkled when they opened the door. They shook the snow off their coats. At first they couldn't see anybody, and then they saw the grocer sitting behind the cash register. But there was no sign of Lasker.

"Are you looking for the gentleman?" the grocer asked.

"Yes," said Walker. "Where is he?"

"I don't know. I had to go to the back of the store. Then I heard the bell, and when I came back he was gone. I thought you'd come and he'd gone out with you."

"How did he look?" Walker asked. "Did he look distraught?"

"Oh, no. He was as pleasant as could be. He just didn't want to talk on the phone."

"Well, thanks," said Walker, and to Alexander Budak he said, "We'd better get back to my apartment. Perhaps he'll show up after all."

19

"I had the strangest feeling of déjà vu," said Alexander Budak as they trudged back through the heavy snow. "That store looked exactly like a little grocery store up in Yellowknife where I once waited for my father. Someone told me he always came there at a certain time, but he never showed up."

Back in the apartment, Walker phoned Lasker's house. He hadn't returned. "Now I got his wife all worried," he said. "She said she'd phone when he got back."

About half an hour later, she phoned. David Lasker had come back. He was terribly sorry, she said. He couldn't wait. Something drove him out of that store. But he did want to see Alexander Budak. Could he come over to Lasker's house next day, around eight in the evening?

Alexander Budak said he would be delighted and Walker passed it on to Lasker's wife.

The next evening was clear and cold. Alexander Budak got a taxi about a quarter to eight. It took about twenty minutes to get to Lasker's house. When he got out of the taxi and looked at the house, it seemed dark. He paid the driver, but told him to wait.

He walked up to the door and rang the bell. No one came to the door. He rang again, leaving his finger on the button for quite a while. He heard the bell ringing, but there was no answer. He checked to see if he had the right house. There was no doubt. Perhaps he had the wrong address. But no. He'd written to Lasker at that address and his letters had arrived. He rang the bell again. He waited. Nothing moved inside. No light went on. Nobody came to the door.

Slowly he walked back to the waiting taxi. Its running motor was the only noise in the street. "Nobody home," he said to the driver. "Strange . . . . You better take me back to the hotel."

About ten days after he came back to Edmonton, he got a letter from David Lasker. When he saw that strange, intricate writing, he got very agitated. It took him several minutes before he felt he could open the envelope.

"It was impossible for me to see you," Lasker had written. "You wanted to ask me things. I have no answers. But you are in my heart. Let me be in your heart also. We had an almost meeting. Perhaps that is not much. And yet it is something. Remember me."

Chassidic Song

Chassidic Song

Huge, full-bearded, the figure stood in the passage-way that separates the first-class from the tourist compartment. His eyes surveyed the compartment carefully, as if to see who was in the plane and how many seats were not yet taken. Arnold Weiss, sitting by a window in the back, felt the eyes upon him. For a moment he was mesmerized. The dark eyes held him. Then they swept past him.

The figure moved slowly into the compartment, a strange, totemic apparition. Incongruous, thought Arnold Weiss. A Chassid on a plane, flying from Montreal to New York. Why strange? And if a nun wearing a black habit and wimple or a priest in a long cassock had come down the aisle, would I have been astonished? Then why now? The long, black gabardine caftan swished softly as he walked.

Behind him now other black-caftaned, black-hatted figures appeared, moved forward. Arnold Weiss counted them. One, two . . . five . . . ten. The first, the tallest, stopped, checked the seat number on his boarding pass, took a step or two, and then sat down beside Arnold Weiss. The others followed, took their seats. All around him now Chassidim sat. Surrounded, thought Arnold Weiss, on all sides. He shifted in his seat. He smiled.

The Chassid beside him took off his broad, round, black hat. Underneath he wore a black skull cap, a *yarmulke*. He adjusted it, then reached deep into the pocket of his caftan and brought out a small, dog-eared Hebrew book and began to read. He stretched one of his legs sideways into the aisle, and Arnold Weiss noticed his high, black boots. All around him the Chassidim talked, some in Yiddish, some in English. The Chassid beside him remained silent, reading his book. Now and then his lips moved, as if he were praying. The seat could barely contain his huge frame.

Quietly, smiling, a stewardess walked through the aisle, looking to see if all the seatbelts were fastened. She stopped. Smiled. Said gently, "Please fasten your seatbelt."

Arnold Weiss instinctively reached for the belt, then remembered that he had fastened it some time ago. Her quiet command was addressed to the Chassid, who put his book on his lap and began to struggle with the two ends of the belt. He had to extend the belt to its full length, and even then barely managed to snap the buckle shut. Impossible, thought Arnold Weiss, that the belt could restrain a frame that was like the trunk of a tree if anything should happen that would really test the strength of the belt.

The plane began to taxi out to the runway. Arnold Weiss felt the man beside him tense up, and the tension communicated itself to him. The engines roared, the plane gathered speed on the ground. The Chassid gripped his book, but his eyes looked to the side, out of the window. The upper part of his body swayed slightly, back and forth. His lips moved.

Now they were airborne. His body relaxed. The tension went out of his face. He looked at Arnold Weiss and smiled. Arnold Weiss returned the smile. Then looked away, out of the window, saw the landscape arrange itself into geometric patterns, the St. Lawrence river cutting through the squares, winding its way east.

"Are you going to a *Farbrengen*?" His head turned away, towards the window, Arnold Weiss heard himself speak, the words shaping themselves almost involuntarily, as if it was someone else's voice that was speaking.

The Chassid looked up from his book. Half-startled, half-puzzled, he cried out, "How did you know that word?"

Arnold Weiss turned towards him. "That word?" he repeated.

"A *Farbrengen*."

"A *Farbrengen*. A *Farbrengen*." Arnold Weiss repeated the word softly, as if he were trying to fathom its strange sound. "I don't know. I don't know how it came into my mind."

"Such a word. So unusual. And you don't know how it came!" There was an undertone of mockery in the voice of the Chassid. "Do you even know what it means, that word. A *Farbrengen*."

Arnold Weiss hesitated. "Isn't it," he ventured at last, "isn't it a — a kind of gathering where Chassidim come together, to eat and to drink, to talk and to listen. And to sing."

"But who told you the word?"

"I don't know any more. I can't remember any more. I haven't heard the word in — God knows how long. Thirty, thirty-five years."

"So. You heard the word. A long time ago. But you heard it. And where did you hear it?"

"I don't know exactly," said Arnold Weiss. "But it must have been in my grandfather's house."

"In Canada?"

"No. No. In Poland. In my grandfather's house. When I was a child."

"You are from Poland?"

"My grandfather lived in Poland. But my mother and father lived in England. My father had gone to England right after the first world war, and then went back to Poland to marry my mother, and brought her to England. I was born there. But from time to time we used to go to Poland to visit my

27

grandparents. And in my grandfather's house I heard about a *Farbrengen*."

"So. And your grandfather. Was he a Chassid?"

Arnold Weiss thought for a while. "I don't know," he said then. "I don't really know. I wasn't aware. We went there in the summer two or three times before he died. In 1932 or 1933. That's when he died."

"So he was spared," said the Chassid.

"Spared? Spared what?"

The dark eyes turned on Arnold Weiss. "You have to ask?" the Chassid said then, with a hint of a reproach in his voice. "Spared what, you ask . . . The war. The Hitlerites. The holocaust."

Arnold Weiss nodded his head. "Yes," he said, his voice suddenly hoarse, his mouth feeling dry. "Yes. He was spared. If you put it that way."

"He must have been a Chassid," the other speculated. "Your grandfather. Or else why would he have talked about a *Farbrengen*?"

"Yes, I suppose," said Arnold Weiss. "He was probably close to the Chassidic movement." For a moment he was sunk in reverie. "He had a long beard," he continued softly. "I used to sit on his knee, and I stroked the beard. I remember that. But I don't think I ever saw him wear a caftan. He didn't wear the — the uniform. The Chassidic uniform." He smiled. But if he expected a smile in return, he was disappointed.

"If he talked about a *Farbrengen*," the Chassid reasoned, as if he were explicating a passage in the Talmud, "then he must have gone to a *Farbrengen* when you heard him talk about it. Or he must have been planning to go to one . . . . Where did he live? Your grandfather. In what town?"

"In Stanislavov."

"Was there a Rebbe in Stanislavov?"

"I don't know."

"I think there must have been," the other asserted. "He must have gone to a *Farbrengen* there. Your grandfather. To be

28

with the Rebbe. To hear the wisdom of the Rebbe. To drink from the fountain. To sing . . . . What was his name?"

"My grandfather's?"

"Yes."

"Moses. Moses Drimmer."

"And yours?"

"Arnold Weiss."

"Do you keep the commandments?"

Impertinence. What right did he have to ask such a question? Out of the blue. Overbearing, he seemed to tower over him, assuming a kind of moral superiority. Arnold Weiss felt pressed against the window. He did not wish to enter into an argument. "What is your name?" he asked, ignoring the question.

"Josef Shemtov," said the Chassid. "I came from Hungary. But after the war. I survived . . . . But I asked you a question. Do you keep the commandments?"

"What is it to you?" Arnold Weiss demanded. His voice rose slightly, though he tried to keep it under control, to keep it calm.

"I think a grandson of Moses Drimmer should keep the commandments," said Shemtov. He spoke as if he had known the other's grandfather and so had a right to question him and to issue moral commands.

"Who says that a man must do what his father did, let alone that a grandson should follow the grandfather?"

"But you sat on his knee and you stroked his beard. So you should honour his memory and keep the commandments."

"What of my father's memory? Perhaps he didn't keep the commandments, and I follow him."

Shemtov would not be deterred. "All the worse," he said. "And even more necessary that you should return to the faith of your grandfather."

Arnold Weiss laughed. He couldn't take him seriously.

But Josef Shemtov persisted. "Don't laugh. Don't laugh. Moses Drimmer hasn't forgotten."

29

"Where is this leading?" asked Arnold Weiss, now clearly irritated. "Why did you start all this?"

"What do you mean — I?" exclaimed Shemtov. "Did I start this? What did I start? Did I talk to you first or did you talk to me first? Did I tell you where I was going? Or did you ask me? Who mentioned the *Farbrengen*? Did I or did you?" He was silent for a moment, lost in thought. Then he said very quietly, "But even did you? Or perhaps it was Moses Drimmer speaking through you. Not the father. The grandfather." He paused, triumphant. The dark eyes challenged Arnold Weiss.

Bemused, but mesmerized almost, Arnold Weiss groped for words, but before he could find what he wanted to say, Shemtov continued.

"The *Rebonoh shel Olem* — the Almighty — blessed be the name — works in very mysterious ways. How could we know that Moses Drimmer — blessed be his memory — who used to sit at the feet of a holy Rebbe and listened to the wisdom of the holy words, and who sang and danced at a *Farbrengen*, would be with us here in a plane and speak through you, his grandson?"

"You are mad," said Arnold Weiss.

"Mad? Who spoke to you? Who whispered to you that word? A *Farbrengen*. When did you ever speak the word before? When did you remember before?" His questions were now challenges. "When?" he demanded.

"You can make a lot out of a little word," said Arnold Weiss, trying to sound very casual, but suddenly feeling eery, as if his grandfather were really here, on this plane, flying from Montreal to New York. He looked about him, turned his head, to see the other Chassidim filling all the seats around him.

"It is not an ordinary word," said Shemtov. "It is a very special word. And you knew it. How long is it since you spoke the word?"

Arnold Weiss cleared his throat. "So far as I know," he said then, "I have not spoken the word in thirty, thirty-five years. Come to think of it, I don't know if I have ever spoken

the word. I heard it, but I don't think I ever used it. But then —
why should I have? I had no reason to."

"But you did. When I saw you, I didn't know you. I had
no intention to speak to you. When you said the word, I was
completely astonished. I didn't even think you were Jewish.
You don't even look like a Jew."

"Because my hair is short and I don't have sidelocks...
peyes... and I don't wear your uniform?" He thought he had
turned the tables on Shemtov. The taunt in his voice
proclaimed his sense of satisfaction.

Shemtov shook his head. His hand reached up and
touched the *yarmulke* on his head. "A soul is bare," he said.
"But so long as we live here we have to wrap up the body. And
what a man wears has to speak also. A man is weak. He has to
remind himself who he is and what he is. Sometimes the burden
is heavy. How easy it would be to sink away into the crowd, to
become like all the others. No one would see. No one would
notice. But no! No no! We cannot do that. We have to show our
faith."

"There are many varieties of faith," said Arnold Weiss.

"Are you faithful?"

"In my fashion."

"When you married — did you marry out of the faith?
Did you marry a *shikse*?"

Arnold Weiss felt the blood rush into his face. "What —
what is this?" he stammered. "What right have you to ask me
these questions? Are you my conscience? Who appointed you?"

Without a moment's hesitation, Josef Shemtov said,
"Moses Drimmer appointed me. The grandfather. I sit for
him."

"Tomorrow," Arnold Weiss said, "I'm going to meet my
wife in New York. She's coming from Vancouver. I was away
for a week — in Montreal. You might say...," he stopped and
smiled, "that I was at a kind of *Farbrengen*. I was at a
conference that was concerned with the work of James Joyce
.... Have you ever heard of him?"

31

Shemtov shrugged his shoulders, non-committal. "But I asked *you* a question."

"He was an Irish writer," said Arnold Weiss. "He was born a Catholic, but one of the great characters he created was a Jew. Leopold Bloom. At this conference I gave a paper that was concerned with Leopold Bloom's Jewishness."

"And your wife?" Josef Shemtov insisted.

"She is Jewish, too," said Arnold Weiss.

"*Gott sei Dank*," said Josef Shemtov, with a great sign of relief.

In the front of the compartment the stewardess had begun to serve a lunch of cold sandwiches. Smiling, she made her way along the aisle, handing out trays. The Chassidim declined. Josef Shemtov looked at Arnold Weiss, waiting to see what he would do. For a moment it seemed as if he would decline also, but then he reached out with a sudden motion and accepted the proffered tray. It contained two sandwiches, one cheese and one ham, and a piece of chocolate cake.

Arnold Weiss sensed the disapproving eyes of Josef Shemtov upon him, but could not bring himself to face him. He began to eat the cheese sandwich, slowly, deliberately. When at last he glanced sideways, he saw that Shemtov had opened his book and was reading. Or was he praying?

Suddenly, he closed the book, but continued to hold it with both his hands. He began to speak very softly. "I was not yet thirteen years old when the Hitlerites stormed through the town where we lived. In a few months I was going to be *Bar-Mitzvah* and I was already learning and preparing. I came from a *balebatische* family, a respectable family. We were orthodox, of course, but we were not a chassidic family. My father was a modern man. There were Chassidim in the town, but we had nothing to do with them. My father thought they were fanatics. I went to the *Gymnasium* in the town, and in the afternoon I went to Hebrew school. I didn't go to the *Yeshivah*, where the chassidic boys went. I knew some of them because I used to meet them, and sometimes we played together, but I thought the way my father did. I couldn't imagine myself dressed the way they were dressed." A thin smile creased the corners of his mouth. "The way I am dressed now . . . . But once the fire started to burn, it didn't make any difference how we were dressed. We trembled and we huddled together. When I came back, the house was empty. I didn't know what had happened. A cold hand pressed my heart. I ran to a neighbour's house. It also was empty. Then I saw a beggar in the street and he told me that soldiers had come and driven them all away. So I was left alone. I hid myself. I begged. I wasn't going to let myself be caught. I slept in forests. I huddled in dark corners.

"Then I was taken in by a *goyische* family. They gave me food and they let me sleep in their house. They had mercy on me, they had *Rachmones*. For this I bless them. So it pleased God to save my life. But I had to pay a price. I had to deny myself. My family. My religion. I went to church with that family. I heard the mass. I made the sign of the cross. I was blessed by the priest."

Beads of perspiration formed on his forehead, and he pulled out a handkerchief that had been tucked into his sleeve and wiped them away. Arnold Weiss had stopped eating. The ham sandwich lay untouched on the tray.

"So I survived," Shemtov went on. "The only one in my family. Why? What reason did the *Rebonoh shel Olem* — blessed be the name — what reason did He have that I should survive? And in such a manner. Only in my heart of hearts I kept the faith, and I prayed that one day it should shine out. When the end of the war came, I was not yet sixteen. I ran away from that town, from that family. I didn't know where I was running. Finally I landed up in a camp. I was caught in a net, like a fish. With hundreds, with thousands of others. They were like me and they were not like me. Now I was free to practice my own religion. To pray in the holy language. Only now everything was bitter. The *Rebonoh shel Olem* deserted me. Of all my family, He had saved only me, and now He deserted me. . . . In the camp when I came there was already a *shul*. Three

33

times a day they prayed there. All day long some sat and learned there. At first I went with a glad heart. After I had denied who I was for so long, I could pray again to my own God in the holy language. Only now my heart was a desert. I couldn't sing. I had no joy when I said the prayers . . . ." He reached for his handkerchief again and wiped the perspiration from his brow. "Why should this happen? Was it a punishment? Was it a test? I didn't know, and I became very bitter and very angry. The *Rebonoh shel Olem* — blessed be the name — had cast me out. He had saved me. And then He had cast me out. Why? How could this be? It was a great, great riddle. But it was a riddle I couldn't solve. So — if He had cast me away, I would cast him away. For ten years, the Presence withdrew itself from me, and I withdrew myself from the Presence. For ten years."

He stopped. It seemed as if he were waiting for Arnold Weiss to say something, but Weiss, stunned by the intensity of Shemtov's words, remained silent.

Shemtov continued. "Then I was scooped up again. Like a stone in a great shovel. With other young people I was sent to Canada. To start a new life. I went to Winnipeg. And there I lived with a nice Jewish family. They treated me like a son. They gave me love. They were wonderful people. Only what did they believe?"

"But they gave you love," Arnold Weiss protested.

"Yes," said Josef Shemtov, "yes, they gave me love. But it wasn't enough. There was still in me a desert, an emptiness. And they couldn't fill it. Deep in my heart of hearts there was a darkness. They sent me to school. I studied. I became an accountant. Then I left Winnipeg and I went to Montreal . . . One day there, on a Friday evening, in the winter, I saw a Chassid. I had never before seen Chassidim in Canada. Not in Winnipeg, and not in Montreal before that moment. He walked in the opposite direction from me. And then suddenly something in me told me — commanded me — that I should turn around and follow him. He went to his *shul* and I went

34

with him. And there that evening, when the Chassidim welcomed the bride of the Sabbath, there was so much joy that I couldn't believe it was possible. I couldn't believe that it was true. God had taken away every reason for singing, and still they sang .... Then suddenly, the Presence entered into me, like a stream. I cried out. I sang. I sang, too. I had no reason to sing, and yet I sang."

A male voice announced, first in English, then in French, that the plane would be landing in New York shortly, and asked all passengers to fasten their seatbelts.

Josef Shemtov fell silent. He fumbled with his belt, fastened it, and opened his book. Arnold Weiss wanted to ask him some questions, but Shemtov's whole bearing now discouraged any further conversation.

Smoothly the plane touched down. Shemtov looked up from his book. "*Boruch Hashem*," he murmured.

The plane came to a halt. People began to move out into the aisle. Josef Shemtov put on his broad black hat. Slowly they moved towards the front of the plane, Josef Shemtov just ahead of Arnold Weiss. As they were about to leave the plane, Shemtov turned round and held out his hand. Arnold Weiss took it.

"*Seit gesund*," Shemtov said. "Remember your grandfather. He knew that the tongue is the pen of the heart, but melody is the pen of the soul." He nodded his head slowly. "He sang. Your grandfather. Oh, yes. He sang, too."

Homecoming

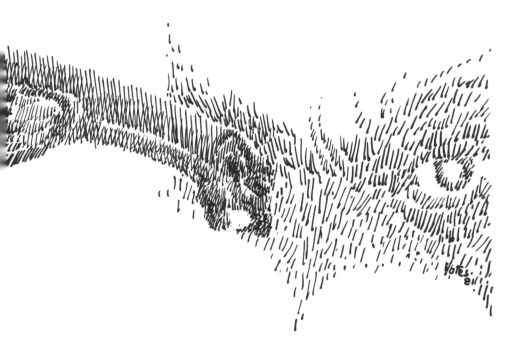

Homecoming
A Memory of Europe After the Holocaust

I

The little dirt road wound along like a moving snake. It was narrow and soggy, and two deep furrows marked the way where a horse-drawn cart had passed. An austere March sun, partly hidden, burst through the slowly-moving cloud banks now and then, transforming grayish-white patches of snow into murky little puddles along the road. But spread across the fields, covering them with a hard, porous, dirty crust, there was still a lot of snow. On both sides of the road tall, bare poplar trees stretched curved branches against the low-reaching sky, and in the distance, scattered irregularly through the fields, a few peasant huts, built of unpainted split logs and covered by old, heavy, rye-thatched roofs, broke the monotonous flatness of the countryside.

A young man was walking along the road, taking slow, even steps, his eyes scanning the landscape intently. He wore an old, gray coat made of coarse cloth and high boots that had once been brown. On his head he had a turret-shaped hat of curly black sheepskin which he had pushed deep down over his ears so that it completely hid his forehead and threw sombre shadows about his eyes. Slung over his left shoulder he carried a dirty brown knapsack which seemed quite empty and sagged

39

against his back.

Towards noon he rested. Taking the knapsack from his shoulder, he walked to the side of the road and sat down beneath a tree, on the driest rock he could find. Then he opened his knapsack and took from it half a loaf of black, hard-crusted cornbread which he began to eat slowly, cutting off small pieces with his pocket knife, as if he were whittling wood.

When he had finished eating he put what was left of the bread into the bag again and leaned back against the tree. After a few minutes, overcome by drowsiness, his head fell forward onto his chest, almost touching his drawn-up legs, and he sat there, hunched up upon himself, slumbering uneasily.

He was awakened suddenly by a sharp, rasping voice that was cursing violently. He roused himself with a start, almost toppling off the stone. Not far from where he was sitting he saw an old peasant furiously beating a horse, trying vainly to get his cart out of a mudhole. The horse was old and bony and, frightened by the curses and hurt by the lash, it strained powerfully, its hide glistening with the perspiration of its labour. But with each pull the rear wheels ground themselves deeper into the soft, muddy ground, and the peasant, growing more furious, lashed out insanely against the beast. The horse, writhing wildly, its hoofs digging deep into the earth, made one last tremendous effort, every muscle stretched taut so that it seemed as if at any moment a bone would break and pierce the hide.

The young man jumped up and ran towards the cart.

"Stop it!" he shouted. "Stop it! You'll kill the horse!"

The peasant did not seem to hear him and he kept on lashing the horse until the young man was directly upon him and pulled him back. Then he turned round and glowered at him with a hostile stare.

"Who are you?" he asked after a while. "Where did the devil send you from to come here interfering with my work?"

"I don't want to interfere with you. But you'll never get your cart out of the mud that way. Have you so many horses

40

that you can afford to kill this one?" He went up to the steaming horse and patted it softly.

"Let me worry about my own horses," the peasant said crossly, his voice filling with stubbornness and anger. "It's my horse, and if I want to beat it I can beat it, and if I want to kill it I can kill it, and it's nobody's business."

The young man shrugged his shoulders. "Go on, then, and kill the horse," he said. "I won't stop you. It's your horse, as you say. But when the horse drops dead, then take the cart and lift it onto your back and carry it to your hut. And if you find that your arms are not strong enough to lift the load, and that makes you angry, go and cut them off. They're your arms, and you can do anything you want with them. Go and cut them off." He lowered his voice and spoke as if he were giving away a dark secret. "There are better ways of using the brains God gave you. And then you can save a fellow creature, and you will come home with your horse pulling your load and your hands holding the reins." He put his left hand into the deep pocket of his coat and fumbled about in it. Then he brought out a cigarette, turned it lovingly in the palm of his hand and broke it in two. "Here," he said, offering one half to the peasant, who was staring at him in utter amazement. "Sit down for a minute and rest yourself. And afterwards I will help you get the cart out of that mudhole."

The peasant pulled his ragged, home-spun coat tightly about him. He was suspicious of the stranger, and he didn't know what he should say. He reached out a reluctant hand, almost snatching the cigarette away, like an animal afraid of being caught in a trap. Then with his ferret-like eyes still resting on the young man, he shambled over to the side of the road and sat down, stretching his legs out before him. He had neither shoes nor boots. His legs were wrapped around thickly with several layers of rags held together by pieces of string, and birch-bark sandals were on his feet.

The stranger came over to him and lit his cigarette. Then they puffed away in silence, enjoying the smoke.

41

"This is the first cigarette I have had in such a long time that I don't remember even when it was," said the peasant. He inhaled deeply. "Real tobacco, not rolled bark. Real tobacco. I forgot how it tasted." He was becoming more jovial now. He kept the smoke inside him as long as he could. His little brown eyes did not for a moment stray from the figure of the young man. They watched him, puzzled and perplexed.

"Where do you come from?" he asked after a while.

There was no answer. Instead, a question. "How far is it to Narodnowa?" He was leaning against a tree with his back to the peasant, and his eyes were turned up towards the sky.

"If you walk and make no stop along the way, you can be there in five hours. I have often walked there in the summer, carrying loads. And then it takes me seven hours. But you are young and you carry nothing heavy. You will be there in five hours."

"It looks like rain," said the young man softly. "Five hours, you say? I'll be drenched to the skin before I get there."

The peasant finished smoking his cigarette. There was only a tiny stub left. He looked at it wistfully and then put it away carefully in a pocket of his smock. "Don't throw away what is left of your cigarette," he said to the young man in a pleading, almost whining tone of voice. "Give it to me. I can still get some tobacco out of it. But you don't need it, for you are a rich man."

The other turned and smiled. "Why do you say that I am a rich man?" he asked.

The peasant took off his cap and scratched his head. "You wear boots on your feet, made of real leather. And then — and then, you have cigarettes, and I think you must have a lot of cigarettes if you are willing to give me half of one."

The stranger laughed out loud. "Surely I am a rich man," he said. "I am rich in sorrows. If I could buy land with sorrows, peasant, then I would have enough to buy the whole world."

The peasant rose slowly to his feet. He tried not to look at the stranger. He was suspicious of him and somewhat afraid.

42

"Tell me," the stranger asked, "when were you in Narodnowa the last time?"

The answer came slowly, haltingly. "It is now a long time. Almost a year. I was there last on the day when the war was over."

Remembrance of the event quickened his tongue and for a moment he forgot his suspicions. "Almost the whole village walked into the town and we danced and drank and cursed the Germans. We stayed there till it was long past midnight. It was a dark night, and I don't know why we began to fight on the way back, for we were all feeling very happy." He shook his head. "And Stanislaus Kaziemiercz was killed with a knife that night and we were all very sorry because he was a good man and people liked him in the village. But otherwise nothing happened, and on the next day we buried him and he had a much better funeral than he would have had if he had died in his bed, for he was a very poor man." He stopped abruptly and suspicion crept back into his voice. "But why are you so interested in Narodnowa?" he asked, glancing sideways at the stranger.

"I knew the town well. I knew it very well. I am going there now to see some people. It was a nice little town. Tell me, did it suffer much when the Germans came here?"

The peasant spat with great contempt. "God's stinking curses upon them," he growled, and his narrow eyes contracted into a leer of hate. "They're in hell now, and the devils are cutting pieces of flesh from their arses . . . . They came here and took away everything we had and then they burned the houses in the villages and drove the young men off like herds of cattle. They robbed the stores in Narodnowa and broke into the houses. They carried away everything and sent it to their bitches and bastards in Germany." He spat again. Then he went on, speaking slowly, savouring his words. "They did only one thing in Narodnowa which was good and joyful to hear." A smile spread slowly over his face and his eyes brightened. "They went into the quarter where the Jews used to live, and first they

43

took everything. Then they threw torches into the nicest houses of the Jews, and you could see the red glow in the sky from where you stand now. Then they started to drive the Jews away, first in small groups, but then more and more at a time until there was not a Jew left in Narodnowa." His voice became glowing. "And now there are not many Jews left in the country because the Germans killed them and gassed them and burned them to death. And that is the only good thing they have done. Now the Germans are gone and the Russians have come, and with them the Communists. Now they sit in the great city of Warsaw, the godless, stinking, accursed bastards, and everybody says that they are going to take away all that we have left."

"You talk too much." The voice of the stranger was suddenly hard and cutting. "You should keep your mouth shut. You say things that it would be better for you not to say. I told you before to use the little brains you have, but perhaps you are too old now, and you never learned while you were young."

The peasant cringed and shied away from him. He mumbled to himself and did not dare to look up from the ground. He waited, cowering like a frightened beast, expecting the stranger to step forward and hit him across the head. He was used to this. The masters for whom he had worked had always punished him like that. But the young man only picked up his knapsack and threw it over his shoulder.

"Why are you so much afraid of the Communists?" he asked. "Why are you afraid that they will take things away from you? What have you got that anybody would want to take away? The rags you wear? That carcass of a horse or your stinking cart?"

When the peasant saw that the stranger was not going to hit him, he dared to raise his eyes from the ground and whispered, "You said for me to rest a while, and you said you would help me to get my cart out of the mud."

The young man looked down at him contemptuously. "I've wasted a lot of time with you already," he said. "I'm sorry

44

now that I said I would help you. The horse is yours, you said. You can kill him if you like, you said. Well, then, go and kill him. Go on and kill him. And then go and dig out the cart by yourself, and if the hole is big enough, lie down in the dirt and bury yourself. And then you will have all the rest you want. You can rest then until the judgement day, if there's any rest in hell." Then he turned sharply and walked away.

The peasant straightened up and watched him go. In his slow brain he was brooding over the things the stranger had said to him. He remembered all the gossip he had heard in the village inn, and the horrible rumours that were circulating round the countryside, and there rose in his mind the lean, sharp-faced figure of Father Wojcieck, haranguing the assembled congregation wildly from the wooden pulpit of the little village church, telling fearful parables and calling up dark images whose terrors had penetrated deep into his consciousness, so that he was never able to obliterate the memory of them. Now he was suddenly sure who the stranger was. Yes, he had heard of him. He was the devil figure Father Wojcieck had talked about so often and so vividly. Now that he knew who the stranger was, he crossed himself hurriedly and he mumbled a prayer to his patron saint, for he was terribly afraid.

He stared after the stranger, who was walking quietly, taking sure, even steps, his eyes straight on the road. Suddenly, obeying an overpowering impulse within himself, the peasant began to run tremblingly after him, calling loudly to him and gesturing wildly with his hands, beckoning him to stop.

The stranger paid no heed to him, and though he turned round and saw the grotesque, rag-tattered figure of the peasant panting towards him, he continued to walk on as if he had neither heard nor seen him. It was only when the peasant came within arm's reach that he turned sharply, facing him, for he was afraid that the peasant, angered by his sudden refusal to help him dig the cart out of the mud, wanted to attack him.

But then an astonishing thing happened. The peasant, his breath coming fast, fell down on his knees before the stranger

45

and clasped him round. For some time neither of them said anything, and the silence was only broken by the heavy panting of the peasant as he was trying to catch his breath. The young man looked down at the crouching figure, completely taken by surprise. He could feel the heaving body of the peasant against his thighs, and he didn't quite know what he should do. At last he pushed him away, more rudely than he had intended, and the peasant fell backward into the oozing sludge of the road.

"What is it? What do you want from me?" the stranger asked, feeling uncomfortable and ill at ease. "Why did you get down on your knees before me?"

The peasant got up slowly. He pulled off his cap and stood there, his straw-dry hair dishevelled, his head bent.

"I know who you are," he said slowly, his voice trembling and monotonous. He did not look up from the ground, but spoke as if he were addressing an impersonal, powerful force.

"Who am I?"

"I know who you are," the peasant repeated. "And now you will go and tell them all I have said, and soon men will come to my hut in the night and take me away. Come with me now to my hut, and I will let you take everything you want to take if you will not tell them what I have said."

"You are a fool," the stranger said softly. "You are a fool. . . . Who do you think I am?"

The peasant remained silent, and the other repeated his question. "Who do you think I am?"

"You are sent to spy on us," the peasant answered, and his voice was so low that the young man had to strain forward to hear the words. "I have heard many things about the spies."

The stranger laughed. He took his knapsack from his shoulder, stood it up on the ground, and leaned forward, closer to the peasant. "What have you got in your hut that would make me want to come with you?" he asked.

The peasant hesitated. He seemed to be turning something over in his mind. At last he spoke. "I have a few chickens, and a cow, and there is still a loaf of bread left from the last baking. I would let you have the chickens and the bread."

There was a pause. Then the stranger said, "I am not a spy. But — let us say I am a spy. Do you think you could bribe me with a chicken or two and a loaf of bread?"

The peasant disregarded him. "Come with me to my hut," he insisted stubbornly.

The stranger stepped forward quickly and grabbed him by the shoulder. "Look at me," he said sharply, but the peasant did not raise his eyes to him. He stood there silently, slightly trembling under his grip. The young man began to feel a kind of pity for the ragged, tattered figure who stood before him like a beast, ignorant and afraid. "Listen to me," he said, and a bit of softness mingled with the hard, metallic tone of his voice. "I am not a spy, and I am not going to send anybody to fetch you in the night. What you said about the Communists is nothing to me. I have nothing to do with them. But what could they take away from you? What have you got that they would want? Chickens and bread? Maybe they might even do something for you. Who has ever done anything for you? As far as I am concerned, you can hate them or you can love them. It is unimportant to me. I have nothing to do with the party or with the government. So it is all the same to me how you feel. But I tell you again that I am not a spy. I am a Jew and I am going back to Narodnowa where I was born. I am going back to see if I can find my mother and my father."

The peasant looked up quickly, peering closely at the stranger, scanning his face. For a moment their eyes met coldly, the little brown ferret-eyes of the peasant, and the tired, brooding eyes of the stranger.

The peasant said slowly, "You don't much look like a Jew." But yet — there was relief in his voice, and his tension relaxed a little.

"I am a Jew. I had to control my temper when you spoke to me about the Jews. I wanted to hit you, but I thought better of it. You are older than I and I didn't want to beat you. And now go about your business and let me go about mine."

The eyes of the peasant filled slowly with a fierce hatred. "If you are really a Jew," he hissed, "I am not afraid of you. Only I am sorry that you are still alive. But if you go to find your mother and your father, you will not find them because they are not there. Their bodies are now rotting away in the earth and the worms have eaten them, or they are burned and their ashes are thrown to the winds." The corners of his mouth widened into a grimace and his whole frame seemed filled with a silent, mocking laughter.

The young man could no longer contain himself. He threw his knapsack down on the ground, out of his way, and stepped quickly up to the peasant. With his left hand he got hold of his smock and pulled him towards himself, and with the flat of his right hand he slapped him twice across the face. Then he slowly relaxed his grip and let him go. He picked up his knapsack and went away quickly, without saying a word. Behind him the voice of the peasant rose to a high pitch and the air was suddenly filled with foul and horrible curses.

The young man never looked back, but he doubled his pace as if he wanted to escape from the curses that were hurled against him. Suddenly he became filled with a strange excitement. He reproached himself for having succumbed to a sudden impulse. He began to walk more quickly, and then he ran, as if someone were pursuing him.

Now he will go and fetch people from the village and they will come after me, he thought.

He broke into a cold sweat and kept on running. Then the feeling of excitement gave slowly way to fear. That was not new to him, for in the past few years he had experienced it often. He had known that sensation when he was hiding from the Germans in a cellar in Warsaw; when he fled the city by night, making his way cautiously through dark alleys and smelly backstreets, through woods and forests, into Russian territory; later, when he fought with a small band of guerillas behind the German lines. It was always the same. First, tense excitement, and then panicky fear, giving way slowly to a period of cool detachment and a kind of nerveless existence.

He could no longer hear the peasant's voice, and he turned round, but the road was empty and only the bare branches of the trees were moving restlessly in the wind.

Nevertheless he decided to approach Narodnowa in a round-about way, and he swerved from the road, cutting across the still snow-covered fields towards the wood.

Once there, he stopped for a moment, feeling shielded and more secure. His mouth was dry and parched. He bent down and picked up a handful of hard-crusted snow and put it to his lips. Strangely enough, he was not hungry, though he'd had nothing hot to eat for two days. But all he wanted was water. Just water.

After half an hour's walk he came upon a brook, still thinly covered by a crust of ice. He knelt down, broke the icy crust, and with a great gasp of relief drank the water from cupped hands. He splashed water over his face, feeling unbelievably revived. The softly gurgling water of the brook calmed him, and he sat there listening to the sound for a few minutes.

The sun had now completely disappeared and a solemn gray was spread across the countryside. He got up from the ground, picked up his knapsack again and began to walk rapidly, trying to make up for the time he had lost by his detour.

Towards five o'clock it began to drizzle, a cold rain mixed with snow. He put his collar up and pushed his hat even deeper into his face. The rain pricked him lightly, like thin needles. And yet he could hardly feel it.

II

Through the haze of the misty twilight the spire of the church rose in the distance, tapering off to a thin point, crowned by the cross. When he first became aware of it, the young man stopped and for several minutes stood gazing, shielding his eyes with his right hand. The thin strings of the falling rain and the monotonous grayness of the oncoming dusk made him think that what he saw was a mirage, for the picture blurred before his eyes, receded tremblingly into a vast expanse of space, then suddenly came back into sharp focus. He walked on, feeling restless and disturbed. There was a force within him that seemed to want to pull him away from the town, and a weak, dull voice made itself heard and whispered to him, Why do you want to go there? What do you expect to find? And it answered its own questions in the same dull, soft, slightly mocking tone, and said to him, Until now you had some hope. But you might find only ruins, and haunting memories of frightful things. Why do you want to find these things?

He had to silence the voice because it threatened to turn him back from his purpose. It is better to know the worst than live forever in doubt, he said to the voice.

Once you know, said the voice, you lose all hope.

I have lost all hope long ago, he said, and there is nothing more to lose. You heard what the peasant said. I must find out, once and for all. There has to be an end if there is to be a new beginning.

After that the voice was quiet and did not bother him any more.

The road was broader now and somewhat less muddy. As he came closer to the town the number of vehicles increased, and he passed several women, wearily trudging along, their backs stooped with bundles of firewood which they had gathered in the forest beyond the town. Now the spire of the church stood out clear and distinct against the sky, so that the gold of the cross could plainly be seen. But suddenly, as he looked at it, it quivered and seemed to vanish into nothingness. And then everything around him, the horse-drawn carts, the dirty, tired stragglers, the road itself, receded and dissolved, shaking off time and space. It was as if he were walking through a dream, seeing things, feeling things, but perceiving them as through a gently-swaying screen of gauze, now very clear, now hazily shimmering, and never quite real.

He entered the town from the south side. The road stretched up-hill, flanked by trees on both sides, and he knew that he would soon pass the big cemetery. He remembered it well, because when he was a child of about six he had once passed this way with his mother and he had wanted to go into the cemetery, but his mother would not allow it. Then he had begun to cry, tugging violently at her arm, and his mother had said sternly, Do you see the big iron fence and the tall spikes all around? Do you know what happens to little boys who want to go in? Do you know what happens to them? Little devils come swooping down and pick them up by the bottom of their trousers and nail them on the tall, sharp spikes.

He shuddered, remembering. It seemed strange now. Why had she said those things? Why would she want to frighten him? Why was she so afraid? Of what? She was not a superstitious person. And yet. Deep fears must have lurked within her.

His mother now entered his waking dream, and he thought he saw her walking beside him, a tall and stately matron, keeping pace with him without apparent effort, briskly and easily. She seemed to observe him critically, her eyes full of concern and worry, yet she never came quite close to him. She walked near the side of the road, and there was an air of coolness and detachment about her. It was a strange picture, not at all like her. But yet she was very real.

He saw her sitting in a tall chair, talking to his father in her soft, firm voice. He couldn't hear what she was talking about, but she seemed very agitated, sometimes making emphatic gestures with her fine hands, and he could see her ring shooting off little sparks when the light caught in it. His father sat quietly, now and again nodding his head, and stroking his pointed little beard. He held a long yellow cigarette-holder in his right hand, turning it lightly between middle and index finger, from time to time lifting it to his lips. The cigarette came to life, glowed a warm red. He exhaled. The blue smoke seemed to shoot out of his mouth, spread slowly, floated in thin waves through the room, filling it, then vanished.

Blow smoke through your nose, Papa. I want to see you blow smoke through your nose.

His father laughed. He inhaled and extended his nostrils slightly, then drove the smoke through them.

The boy clapped his hands in delight. His mother motioned him away impatiently. She went on talking. His father rarely threw in a word. She dominated the conversation. After a while his father rose and left the room. He was now alone with his mother. She talked to him. He shook his head. Her voice rose. She was usually gentle, but she could be hard and stern when she wanted to. He stamped his foot defiantly on the floor in an obstinate gesture of refusal. She commanded. He slunk from the room, still defiant, still stubborn.

Curious, he thought, walking along the road in a half dream, how real the gestures were, how real the figures. But what did his mother say to him? He could not hear the words. But sometimes he could hear them. Only not now.

Where did his sister come from? She entered suddenly. He had not seen her come in. The door was closed. Had she come through the window? She talked to him. And now he could hear the words. His and hers. He wore long trousers and smoked a cigarette. So he was grown up. How had he grown up so quickly?

I know why you've come, he said. You've come to talk to me about Mother. I regret the scene. It was ridiculous of me to become so excited. It won't happen again. I won't let it happen again. I promise you.

You said that before. And I thought we had an understanding. Didn't we? And yet you broke that understanding.

I know, he said. But does it really matter? What games

are we playing? Mother knows that her ideas are no longer my ideas. I don't want to argue with her. But sometimes I cannot keep quiet.

You must, when you are at home. That was our understanding. She's tolerant enough in her own way. She doesn't care what you do when you are away at University. But at home it's different. All those strange and heretical ideas of yours. You seem to taunt her with them. Why do you do it?

I'll reform, he said, and laughed.

His mother kept walking beside him, tripping lightly, as if she were dancing, her feet hardly touching the ground. She did not say anything, and that was strange. It wasn't at all like her. There was much about him that she could not possibly like — his unkempt appearance, the sweaty, three days' growth of stubble that covered his face, his dirty, mudcaked boots. But she said nothing. Not a word. Silently she floated at his side. Then she vanished suddenly, without a stir, without a rustle, like a ghost.

He stopped and stared at the empty space. He shook himself, rubbed his eyes, laughed uneasily.

He was now on top of the hill and the cemetery stretched on his left, row upon long row of wooden crosses and gravestones, and tall trees standing guard over the graves. The big iron fence, however, was no longer there. The cemetery seemed to jut out into the road, becoming a part of it.

No barrier divided the dead from the living.

It took a while for him to become fully aware that the fence was no longer there. The tall, sharp spikes were gone. Melted down, he thought, and long since shot off. How many people had been killed?

A sad smile spread over his face. Now I could walk into the cemetery and I would be safe from the little devils, he thought. Or would I? Perhaps they are now everywhere. No longer just in the cemetery. Everything he saw and felt had about it a curious texture of abstraction and unreality. It merely grazed his consciousness, and then evaporated, like steam escaping from a boiling kettle, leaving no trace of its substance.

One part of him said, I have passed here before and my mother told me stories about little devils and I was afraid, and the other asked, When? Where? How?

Yet he clearly recognized the streets that would lead him into the centre of the town. Everything seemed unchanged, as if he had only left yesterday and was returning today, as if there had not been an interval of almost seven nightmarish years.

It seemed as if Narodnowa had not been touched. The war had passed it by. There were no signs of devastation. No vast heaps of rubble, no hollow, burned-out buildings, no bomb-craters in the middle of the streets. Perhaps nothing was changed here. Perhaps his parents were still living in their old apartment. Narodnowa was such a small town, so insignificant, so unimportant.

But the peasant had said that the Germans had driven all the Jews from the town. What did he know? He was ignorant. He had said they had burned the nicest houses of the Jews. But why only those houses? Why had they not burned other houses? Why did the houses stand here along the streets he was passing now? In other towns the invaders had not been so merciful. They had burned and destroyed and killed without provocation.

In Narodnowa, the peasant had said, they had only robbed. A kind of miracle, then. Then the Jews were perhaps also spared by the miracle. His parents certainly. After all, his father was a doctor, and doctors had always been badly needed.

His parents were alive! Of course, they were alive, hoping for him to be alive, too, waiting for him to come home, praying for him to come home!

Yes, he was alive, he was well, he had survived! He was coming, he was coming home! This was the homecoming! Another half hour. After all the years, now only one half hour, and he would be home!

It was still drizzling, and not many people were in the

54

streets. The church was only minutes away, almost within reach of his arms it seemed, and the spire was no longer so dominating and imposing as it had been from the far distance.

He turned into the market-place and looked up at the church. From a niche in the tower two gargoyles stared down at him, their eyes screwed up curiously, their lips pursed into a scoffing pout, their bodies twisted and warped like a misshapen root.

He was fascinated. They seemed to draw him towards them as if by a powerful magnet, beckoning to him to come closer, and mocking him even as they beckoned.

He walked slowly nearer. They drew him inexorably closer, and yet he hated them. He hated their deformity, their monstrousness, the insolence of their grimacing faces, and yet there was also something attractive in their very ugliness. He kept his head turned up towards the tower.

When I was a boy, I was afraid of you, he thought. I never dared even to look at you. I thought you would come down from your tower and do me harm. But I am no longer afraid. Ugliness no longer repels me. I have seen ugliness so revolting that you seem beautiful. And your ugliness is remote, it cannot touch me, you cannot come down from your niche.

The gargoyles laughed derisively, threw back their heads in a convulsive fit, screwed their eyes deeper into their sockets.

He walked up the steps of the church, keeping his eyes fixed on the carved figures in the tower, as if he meant to challenge them.

Suddenly the gargoyles freed themselves from their pedestal and stepped forward, out of the niche. For a moment they hung suspended in mid-air, twisting and squirming, contorting their ugly bodies into fantastic shapes. But they did not swoop down on him. They seemed nailed to the air. He kept his eyes unwaveringly on the two figures, more fascinated than ever, not at all afraid, waiting for them to swoop down on him, prepared to encounter them.

55

Suddenly a hand was thrust forward, gnarled, hooked fingers almost touching his mouth. He reeled backwards, staggered down a few steps, then caught himself on the balustrade. Raising his head, he saw a beggar crouching on the topmost step where the protruding portico shielded him from the rain. His hand was still stretched out.

"Alms for the poor, master," the beggar whispered.

"I need alms myself," he answered, breathing heavily, his hand clutching the balustrade. "I have nothing to give."

The beggar withdrew his hand, crouched deeper into his corner, and let his head fall forward onto his chest.

The young man lifted his eyes slowly to the tower. The gargoyles were back in their niche. Nothing was changed. He was amazed at the absurdities his brain could foist upon him, and he began to laugh, a stertorous, fitful, nervous laughter.

The beggar craned his scraggy neck forward, screwing it out in short thrusts, like a turtle. "Why do you laugh in the presence of God?" he cried out. "This is a place of God. Only the devil laughs when he is in a holy place."

The young man stopped laughing and pointed his finger up towards the gargoyles. "You know the two figures in the tower," he said. "Did you ever see them coming out from their places and hanging in the air?"

The beggar began to tremble. He pressed closer into his corner and with his gnarled left hand he crossed himself three time. "Jesus Christ and Virgin Mary and holy Joseph and all good angels preserve me," he mumbled. "Leave me lying here in peace. When the two figures come down it's a sign that the great judgement day is near. It's a sure sign and they'll come down to search out all sinners. God preserve me from such a sight."

"So I was told, too, when I was a boy," said the young man. "Our teachers told us that in school. And now I tell you that the great judgement day is very near. For when I walked up the steps I saw the figures come out of their niche and they twisted and squirmed and hung in the empty air. But now they are back again, just as they were before. Look up and see."

The beggar trembled. He rose slowly, gathering up the rags that clothed him. Grabbing hold of the railing, he slid down the steps more than he walked, stopping for a moment as he came parallel with the young man, mumbling incantations and charms, and casting spells upon him. Then he averted his eyes and hurried past him. At the foot of the stairs he turned once more, traced a large, trembling cross in the air, and shuffled off like one possessed.

The young man looked after him. He felt sorry that he had frightened him. Once more he looked up at the tower. The gargoyles were safely back in the niche. So the judgement day was not yet at hand, he thought. Then he turned and went slowly down the steps.

It was quite dark now, and only a dimly-glowing lamp in the centre of the market-place threw a pale circle of light onto the wet-glistening cobblestones. He crossed over to the other side. He saw things very clearly now, no longer as through a screen of dreamlike unreality. He wanted to walk quickly, but his feet, suddenly heavy as lead, seemed to drag him down. He felt them, tender and swollen, rubbing against the hard, unyielding leather of his boots. And then he suddenly felt the knapsack on his back pressing hard against his shoulders, weighing him down, as if all the heaviness of his heart and all the sorrows of his young life had accumulated in it. He shifted it onto the right shoulder, but the relief was only momentary. Everything in him cried out for rest. He longed to immerse his body in warm water, ever renewed, flowing over him gently, filling his whole being, soothing and relaxing.

People passed him and he overheard snatches of talk. He envied them. They are going home, he thought. They will sit by the fire and warm themselves in front of it. And then they will go to bed, stretching out on a soft, deep mattress. The thought of this moment of ease and comfort overwhelmed him. On the bed now, on the mattress, there were two bodies, a man and a woman, touching in the dark, caressing, embracing. It was so marvellous that it was almost unbearable.

Now I am going home, he thought suddenly. I, too, am going home! The thought brought forth a feeling of great elation and optimism, and made him walk faster, hurrying to rush home, out of the darkness into the light, out of the cold into the warmth, to end all sorrow and to have rest.

Rest rest peace in peace rest warm water laving my tired body.

And then, coming on slowly, worming its way into his consciousness, the figure of the peasant was before him, small, crouching.

The coarse voice whispered, They are not there, they are not there. Burned, burned, and ashes thrown to the winds. Joyful to hear, joyful to hear, joyful to hear.

He had to stop, and he pressed his hand against his stomach, as if to strangle the apparition and silence its terrible murmurings.

But now his joy was all gone, and he walked very slowly, wishing for something to happen that would make it impossible for him to go where he knew he had to go and was now afraid of going.

A dog came running up behind him and circled round him, barking hoarsely. He tried to kick the mongrel, but missed him. The dog shied away from him and kept on barking, and after a while drew close again. He sniffed at the young man's trousers, yapping lightly, his tongue hanging out of his mouth, his flanks heaving. He lowered his head and began to lick the muddy left boot. He opened his mouth, trying to sink his teeth into the leather, but before he could do it the other boot caught him deep in his side and he dashed off wildly across the street, yelping.

The young man watched him warily. He saw him trotting slowly towards him again, and bent down to pick up a stone. When the dog was quite close, he took aim and hit him straight between the eyes. For a moment the dog stopped barking and stood quite still, and a thin trickle of blood oozed from his mouth. Then suddenly he let out a long, sorrowful wail, almost like the cry of a child, but still he did not move. The young man felt pity for him, and he was sorry that he had hit him. He went up to the dog and squatted down by him, and the dog did not run away. When he stretched out his hand the dog, whimpering softly, licked it with his tongue, and when he got up to walk on, the dog trailed after him.

He was glad now that he had hit the dog because it had relieved some of the tension in him, and his head was clear. His excitement grew again, hope and fear mingled, and he was afraid that his conflicting emotions would tear him apart. He tried hard to keep control over himself, to steel himself against himself, and he kept thinking, Whatever I find, it will at last be the end of uncertainty. To know even the worst is better than not knowing at all.

Through the rain and through the dusk he glimpsed the corner of the street where he had once lived, and from the distance he could plainly see that the house there on the corner was still standing.

A wild feeling of joy surged up in him. He ran. He would soon be able to touch the house.

But when he came close, he saw that there was no house to touch. There was only a mangled, gutted structure. There was no street, only heaps of rubble and bits of rugged slabs of wall set over the rubble heaps, marking them, like rough-hewn gravestones.

And then for a moment everything was blotted out and he could see nothing. A cold hand gripped his heart and pressed it and pushed upward, choking him, and his cry remained stifled in his throat. He felt something rubbing itself against his legs and opened his eyes and saw that it was the dog. An insane fury overcame him, and he turned viciously against the dog and chased him off. He wanted no witnesses, not even a dog.

For a long time he stood there, unable to move, as if he were rooted to the ground. His eyes did not want to see, and yet he could not prevent them from seeing; his brain did not want to know, and yet he could not prevent it from knowing.

This is how it ends. This is how it ends. This is how it ends. Endlessly the words revolved round his mind. All my dreams and all my hopes. This is how it ends. No light, no outstretched hand of greeting, no kiss of welcome. A gutted block of buildings, a pile of rubble half-cleared, a bit of wall left standing, a few gaping holes for windows. This is how it ends. This is the end of my long road. This is the end the end the end . . . And with a terrifying hopelessness he realized that the end was not the end. It was a terrible beginning. He did not want to begin. He did not want to come to terms with what he had now discovered.

His body felt numb, as if his nerves had been anaesthetized. Only his stomach distended and contracted in short and painful spasms. He let go of his knapsack and it dropped down on the ground. He was not aware of it and for some time he kept his hand up near his shoulder-blade and his fist closed as if he were still gripping his knapsack.

Just ruins just ruins just ruins. I'm used to ruins. All Europe is in ruins. Always the same ruins. Destruction is destruction everywhere. All ruins are the same ruins. Ah! But this is a special destruction and these are special ruins. My ruins, not someone else's ruins, my own destruction, and under the rubble perhaps the man who fathered me and the woman who bore me. And my sister, too. I played with her and quarrelled with her and loved her. And where is she now? Where are they all?

He opened the palm of his hand and closed it. Opened it and closed it. Looked at it. The knapsack? Where was the knapsack? Why did the hand open and close and why did the knapsack not drop down on the ground? He looked about for it, found it lying behind him and picked it up. Then he walked on slowly, treading cautiously, as if he were afraid of destroying something, as if it were important that each stone be left exactly where it was, an eternal reminder of chaos and havoc.

The drizzling rain kept falling, regular, monotonous, thin.

Six years and not yet cleared. Tomorrow I'll clear it, make it clean, wipe away the memory, build the houses again.

My ruins, the ruins of my father's house.

He brushed against a piece of standing wall. His hand touched the wall, caressed it.

This is my welcome, the hand extended to grasp mine. This is what is left of my home. A bit of wall, stones, pieces of brick, an odd bit of slate.

He felt the wall, damp and rough against his hand. The sharp edges cut into his flesh and made the blood come. He felt the pain, and he was glad. It was good to feel the pain. It released the tension and allowed feeling to come pouring forth. His body was no longer numb, the pain from the hand spread all through it. And then suddenly tears came welling up and he pressed his body close against the wall, his arms extended as if he meant to embrace it, his lips touching it as if he meant to kiss it. Then he slumped against the wall, crying softly, noiselessly, without a whimper, without a sob.

Two men passed by on the other side, looked briefly at the figure hazily outlined in the deep dusk, and passed by. They thought it was a beggar, starved, cold, and weakened, laying himself down to die.

He did not move. He lay perfectly still, his head touching the wall, weeping through closed eyes. There was no suffering now, no pain, no anguish. There was only the stinging sensation of hot tears coursing slowly down his cheeks, and the cool, humid dampness of the wall against his forehead.

Now there is peace, now there is rest. Now I have come home to rest and to have peace forever.

The wall was like a wet piece of linen, cool and soothing. He lifted his head and leaned his flushed and feverish cheeks against the stone, first one and then the other.

A piece of wall. A piece of stone. Now I can lie here, and yet I cannot lie here. I have come to the end of the road, but it is not really the end of the road. I am in limbo. Neither the end nor the beginning. But I cannot move. My legs will not carry me further now. I must lie here, waiting. Yes, waiting. But for what?

Surely my mother will come to me now, for she must know that I am here, waiting. There is blood on my hand.

Why is there blood on my hand? Why does she not come to me? If she does not come to me, then I must go and seek her. But I cannot move. I am cold and wet and lonely. And there is blood on my hand. I must try and get up and search for her.

He began to grope about in the moist ground with his hand, digging his fingers into the earth, picking up a dark-brown lump of wet earth and crumbling it slowly in the palm of his hand, then letting small pieces of earth fall through his slightly-spread fingers. He put his hand on the ground again, wanting to pick up more earth, but he did not bring it up immediately. He felt something slimy and mucous trying to crawl onto his hand. He wanted to see what it was, and he laid his hand down as flatly as he could, making it easier for the thing to crawl on. He felt it lift what must be its head, exploring his flesh, then wriggling onto the hand, drawing its long, slimy, legless body after it. He shivered, imagining the thing to be something unspeakably loathsome. He did not look down at his hand, but brought it slowly up to the level of his eyes where he could see the worm writhe and bend, twisting its transverse furrows, its body-rings narrowing and expanding.

Only an earthworm, he thought, and he was disappointed, only a blind, helpless, squirming earthworm, not a terribly disgusting reptile, frightful and sickening, fitting the time and the place. He grasped the worm with two fingers and let it dangle in the air, watching it twist and squirm.

Shake hands with the worm. It bids you welcome. It has come crawling out of the earth to greet you. A good worm, a blind worm, perhaps even now come from feasting on your father.

Cold shivers ran down his spine and revulsion rose in him. Furious and angry, he flung the worm aside, hurling it far from him. Then he scrambled to his feet, something within him driving him away from this place which seemed suddenly cursed and haunted, full of memories and ghosts of a past he did not want to encounter.

It was dark now and he could hardly see where he was going. His feet seemed to be on fire, and each step caused him intense pain. He walked aimlessly, not knowing where he might find people who could help him.

He was now in the oldest part of the ghetto, dragging himself forlornly through narrow, deserted, cobble-stoned alleys, passing by dilapidated, unlighted houses whose low brick walls shut out all air and exuded a mouldy odour. From the deep, scummy gutters where streams of dirty water had turned the ground into loose black mud there rose a reeking stench, foul and stale.

Oh, for the touch of a warm human hand, he thought longingly, and for the sound of a kind, reassuring voice.

But there was no movement, no stirring, except the unvarying, interminable patter of the wearisome rain, and from afar came the howling of dogs, calling and answering each other.

He kept close to the houses, supporting himself against the walls, trying to take the full weight of his body off his legs. His feet were aflame, as if all the devils and all the inmates of hell had come to hold a merry celebration in his boots.

Then suddenly he saw the thin figure of a woman detach itself from one of the dirty court-yards and step out into the street. She came scurrying towards him, without seeing him. He hailed her in a low, friendly tone of voice. She let out a short, startled cry and stood for a moment, staring at him. Then she tore herself away, turned sharply and ran off.

He became desperate. "Don't run away from me!" he called after her. "Please don't run away from me."

She did not stop. He began to run after her. She could not keep up her pace, and he caught up with her and grabbed hold of her arm. She tried to wrench her arm away from him, her breath coming short and heavy.

"I've done nothing wrong," she whimpered. "I've done nothing. Let me go! Please let me go!"

He looked into her gaunt, line-drawn, prematurely aged face. Fear, fear, he thought, everywhere I go I meet fear and blind superstition. God, God, he wanted to cry out, when will it end? When will we be rid of our fears?

"Don't be afraid," he said softly, trying to reassure her. "I don't want to hurt you. I only want to ask you what has happened here. I don't want to hurt you."

"Let me go," she cried. "Look, I have nothing you can take away from me. What do you want from me? Let me go."

"I'll let you go," he said. "I want nothing from you. I only want somebody to talk to." He pleaded with her. "First talk to me, and then I'll let you go. I must know something, and perhaps you can tell me. Are some people still alive here? This used to be the Jewish section of the town. My family once lived in this town, not far from where we are standing. Tell me, is anybody left living among the people who lived here before the war? Is anybody left living among the Jews?"

When she heard him ask this question in a trembling voice, she grew calmer and more composed. "A few have come back," she answered slowly. "A very few. More dead than alive." Then after a short pause she asked, "Who are you?"

"I have just come back, too," he said. "But I have found only ruins where our house used to be."

"You said your family once lived here," she said.

"Yes," he said, "and I found the house I lived in burned to the ground."

"What is your family's name?" she asked.

"Drimmer," he said. "And my name is Mordecai. Mordecai Drimmer."

He took his hand from her sleeve, and for a while they stood facing each other in silence.

At last she asked, "Who was your father?"

"My father's name was Aaron," he said quietly. "He was

a doctor. Many of his patients lived in these houses."

She let out a sharp cry. "Aaron Drimmer! The doctor! You are the doctor's son?" She groped for his hand and grasped it tremblingly with her own.

"You knew him?" he asked. "You knew my father?"

"Everybody knew your father," she said simply.

He nodded his head. Slowly and with painful difficulty he brought himself to ask the crucial question. "Is he alive? Is my father alive?"

She did not answer immediately.

"Is my mother alive? And my sister? Have you seen them? Have you heard anything about them?"

"Your father and your mother have not come back," she said slowly. "And I don't know your sister, but I haven't heard her name mentioned. So perhaps . . . . But your father and your mother have not come back to the town. I would know if they had."

His heart sank. A great chasm opened up before him and he felt himself falling into its yawning depths and there was no end to his fall.

The woman recalled him. He heard her say tenderly, "Perhaps your father will come back. He must know that people need him. Perhaps your mother will come back. Perhaps all your family will come back. Every day a few people come back, and it is always like a miracle to us who are here already. When you told me before that you had come back this evening, it was to me as if someone had risen from the dead."

He put up his hand. "I don't want you to think of me like that," he said. "It would be cruel if the dead had to rise from their graves to find what I had to find this evening."

"It would not be cruel," she snapped angrily. "I wish my husband would rise from the dead and come back to me."

He looked past her into the darkness of the street. "If I were dead," he said softly, "and someone brought me back to life, I would not thank him. I would hate him for all eternity."

She drew back against the wall of the house. "Don't talk

like that," she said. "Please don't talk like that. You frighten me."

He reached out his hand and touched her lightly. "Forgive me," he said. "I didn't want to frighten you. I was talking out of my own bitterness, and I was thinking only about myself."

"My husband would not hate me if I could bring him back," she said proudly. "Even if he had to suffer new agonies, he would come back, because he would not want me to be so alone." He saw her eyes fill with silent tears, and she lifted a corner of her shawl and wiped them away. "Only a few weeks," she said softly. "We were married only a few weeks before we were torn apart."

"Perhaps he will come back," he said.

She did not respond to him.

He asked awkwardly, "Where did you come from when I first saw you?"

She stiffened and a sudden coldness crept into her voice. "Why do you ask me? What business is it of yours?"

Fear and suspicion, he thought, fear and suspicion. Trust has vanished from the earth.

"It's none of my business," he said quickly, lifting his hand in protest. "None at all. I didn't mean to be inquisitive."

"It's not a secret," she said. "I was coming from the courtyard over there. In the cellar of that house there is a bakeshop. I thought they were baking tonight, and I wanted to get some bread. But it is all dark. They are not baking, because they have no flour."

"Is there enough food?"

"Too much to starve and not enough to live."

"Black market?"

"If you have money."

"How many people have come back?"

She shrugged her shoulders. "I don't know," she said. "It's hard to say. Perhaps a hundred. Perhaps two hundred. Not more. A lot leave again. They say there's more work in the

66

bigger cities. And some people don't want to stay in Poland any more. They want to go far away. Away from all the memories. To America. Or to Palestine. They say there is some kind of underground organization that helps people."

"How long have you been here?"

"About two months."

"And are you going to stay here?"

"I don't know. I am waiting."

"Waiting for what? For your husband to come back?"

She remained silent. Tears came again and coursed down her cheeks and she did not wipe them away.

"Has the community organized itself?" he asked. "Is there somebody who is looking after things?"

She nodded her head. "David Mantel," she said. "He has organized a community office to try and help people when they come back, and to talk to the government officials."

The name electrified him. "David Mantel!" he gasped. "David Mantel is alive! Where? Where is he? Where does he live? Come, come! Show me where he lives." He took hold of her arm and pulled her towards him.

"Do you know him?" she asked. "Do you know David Mantel?"

"Yes," he cried, full of excitement. "I know him. He — he is my uncle. My mother's brother. Where does he live? You must know where he is. Come, show me where he is. Please show me."

"He lives on Planty Street. Number 2," she said. "I know because it is the community house now. He uses one room for himself, and I think his is the first door on the second floor of the house."

"I've forgotten where the street is," he said, "and I don't know how to find it. Come with me and show me where it is."

She shook her head. "Don't ask me to do that," she said. "In the daytime I would come with you, but not now, not at night. It's so dark and lonely in the streets. I would be afraid to walk back alone. It's not safe to walk in the streets after dark.

During the past few weeks bands of young hoodlums have been roaming around the streets and they've beaten people up when they've caught them in the streets. So people don't go far from where they live after the dark comes on. That's why I was so frightened when you called to me . . . . But Planty Street is easy to find. Go to the end of this street and then turn to your right and walk three more blocks. The third is Planty Street."

"Where do you live?" he asked.

"I live here on this street. Only a few houses away," she said, pointing her finger. "That's why I came out. It was worth the risk. If I had only been able to get some bread . . . . Will you be able to find Planty Street?"

"I'll find the street," he said.

He was quiet for a few moments. Then he said, "I have a piece of black cornbread left in my knapsack. I want to give it to you, so you won't have come out for nothing."

"Bread!" she cried out incredulously. "Bread! But don't give it away. Keep it for yourself. You will be hungry and you will want it yourself."

"I'll manage," he said, groping about in his knapsack. He found the bread and brought it out of the bag. "It's less than I thought," he said, smiling apologetically. "But it's all I have left."

She took the bread and hid it in the folds of her shawl to preserve it from the rain. "God bless you," she said.

He inclined his head lightly towards her. "I don't know what I would have done if I hadn't met you here in the street. I was lost and didn't know where to go. And then you told me that David Mantel is alive! I felt that a miracle had happened."

She smiled.

"I didn't ask you what your name was," he said.

"Rachel," she said. "Rachel Pokorny." Then, after a pause, "Perhaps I will see you again."

"Probably," he said. "Perhaps another miracle will happen. Perhaps your husband will come back."

She looked up at him. He could see her eyes shining in the

darkness. "No," she said slowly. "He will not come back." Her voice was inexpressibly sad. "Only the living can come back. I found out a week ago that he is dead."

"But how can you be sure?" he cried in anguish.

"Someone came back last week. He was with him. In one of the camps. He saw him die."

"But he could be wrong," he said. "How can he be so sure it was your husband who died? It could have been someone else. There are miracles. You said so yourself. Your husband will come back. You are waiting for him. He will come back."

"No," she said, and her voice was quite firm, bereft of all illusion. "He will not come back. I know that he is dead, and the dead don't rise from their graves."

He reached out his hand and stroked her cheek gently. Then he folded his arms around her and embraced her and felt her body trembling against his.

For some minutes they stood together, so. Then she freed herself from the embrace, turned quickly and, without saying a word, hurried away.

He stood watching her until she disappeared into the courtyard of the house where she lived, and then he, too, hurried on, almost running in spite of the pain each step caused him.

The way seemed endless, the goal impossible to reach, like trying to grasp at low-hanging clouds. But David Mantel was alive! At least that was true. And what if it was not? But why should she have mentioned his name? What if it was another man by the same name? No, that couldn't be. It had to be his uncle, his mother's brother.

He will know where my mother is. At least somebody is alive who can connect the present with the past, at least one familiar face among all the strangers, one friend left amid the chaos and the desolation.

Three streets. Only three blocks. Three streets away. But that can be as far as eternity . . . . The devils are dancing a mad waltz in my boots, and if I don't come to Planty Street soon, I

69

won't get there at all. I'll collapse in the street. The devils will out-dance me and bring me down. She said three blocks. Three streets . . . . One block I have already walked. Two blocks. Two streets . . . . One more street. One more block . . . . What will he say when he sees me?

He tried to run, but he couldn't. There was a sharp pain in his side, and his feet seemed to be on fire. He had to slow his pace. It was as if he were walking on glowing coals.

I can't go on much longer, and one block can be as long as a thousand miles. But now I must be close to the house. Only a minute longer. Count till sixty. The devils are dancing like mad.

This must be the house. Number 2. Weary and stooped, he limped up the wooden stairs, holding on tightly to the crumbling, worm-eaten banister, drawing himself up step by step.

The first door on the second floor of the house. That is what she had said. The first door on the second floor the second floor on the first door the first on the first on the second on the door the devils are dancing on the first door on the second floor.

Dimly he perceived the wooden door on the top of the stairs. He lifted his right hand and began to knock on the door, slowly, mournfully, as if he were beating out the rhythm to an unheard funeral march.

Inside all remained silent. Nothing moved, no one stirred. A feeling of blind panic began to overwhelm him. David Mantel is not living here! Has she told me a lie? But why would she do that? She had no reason. Perhaps she was mistaken. Perhaps this is not the right house or the right door.

He began to pound harder on the door. Then he began to shout, "David Mantel! David Mantel! David Mantel!"

And when there was still no answer and no one came to the door, "Mordecai is here! Mordecai! Your nephew! Uncle David! Open the door! Open the door! Open!"

Now there was an excited shuffling of footsteps behind the door, but he did not hear it. Nor did he hear a trembling

70

voice ask, "Who is it? Who is it? Who is it?"

He kept on pounding his fist against the door mechanically, furiously, raising his voice above the din of his own insane tattoo and shouting, "I'm Mordecai! Mordecai! Open the door!"

"Mordecai?" asked the voice behind the door, loud and insistent, "Mordecai?" Now he could hear it. "Mordecai Drimmer?"

"Yes," he cried. "Mordecai Drimmer. Open the door. Let me come in."

He let his arm sink down, exhausted. His body stiffened, his nerves were stretched almost beyond endurance. Then he heard a bolt being pushed back, and the door was opened. A small, thin man stood facing him. His face was pale, his hands were trembling.

For a long moment the two men stared at each other in great consternation and disbelief, as if neither could comprehend that the other was actually standing there before him, breathing and alive.

At last David Mantel drew Mordecai into the room and closed the door. He took his knapsack from him and put it down on the floor. He helped him to take off his heavy, rain-soaked coat. They moved silently, slowly, as if they were in a dream. Then suddenly, as if he were only now grasping the reality of Mordecai's presence, David Mantel flung his arms round him and embraced him and kissed him and kept calling out his name again and again and again.

"Mordecai!" he cried, over and over again. "Mordecai! Alive! Alive!" Tears were streaming down his face.

Mordecai tried to force a smile. "Alive," he said. "After a fashion."

"God be thanked," said David Mantel. "You have come back."

"And the others?"

"The family?"

"Yes. The family."

71

David Mantel spoke very quietly. "No one else has yet come back. I am trying to find out what has happened to them. But for the moment it is very difficult. There is too much confusion. Perhaps some have survived. We must pray and we must hope. You have come back, and I have come back. And perhaps they will also come back. We must wait and we must have patience. We must have trust in the Almighty."

"We have had too much trust," said Mordecai sharply. "We have had too much patience. We have waited too long."

"We must not give up. Especially not now."

"Why should we want to go on living? What point is there in life when so many have been killed and so much has been destroyed?" He felt inexpressibly weary. Nothing mattered any more.

Suddenly all his strength drained from his body. The walls of the small, bare room began to close in on him, and then he himself seemed to be whirled about, ever more swiftly, until he seemed to be floating upwards and upwards, through the ceiling and out of the room. Strange sounds assailed him, and then he heard someone calling his name, but from far, far away, and when he tried to answer, no sound came. He floated further and further away and all was dark and silent.

III

For five days the fever raged in him. From time to time he saw figures hovering above him as he lay on the hard, narrow bed. Sometimes it was the face of a man that he saw, sometimes that of a woman, but he could not make his eyes focus long enough to make out their features clearly before everything dissolved again, and his body floated off into space.

On the sixth day he heard someone call his name out clearly, and when he opened his eyes he saw a thin man whose sad, drawn face looked down at him.

"Mordecai!" said the man. "Mordecai! Can you see me?"

Mordecai had difficulty shaping the words he wanted. "I think — I see," he said at last, slowly.

"And do you know who I am?"

"You are — I think you are — you are — my uncle. My uncle David."

"Thank God, thank God," David Mantel cried out. "You have come back to us." Tears welled up in his eyes. He sobbed. "You have come home. You have come home."

Mordecai's eyes closed. He could not keep them in focus. He was very tired. But things did not dissolve, his body did not float off into space. After what seemed a long, long time he opened his eyes again. David Mantel had pulled a chair up to the bed and was sitting there, looking at him.

"Who else has come home?" Mordecai asked. He didn't have so much difficulty now shaping the words.

"You have come. We must be thankful for that."

"And the others? My mother? My father? My sister?"

A long silence. Then, his voice hardly audible, "No. Not yet."

"And your wife, my aunt Rebecca? And your sons, my cousins?"

"Your aunt and your cousin Jonathan...." His voice broke. Tears were streaming down his cheeks. "They will not come back. They — they have perished."

The words were barely whispers and yet their force was that of hammer blows.

"How — how do you know? How can you be sure?"

"I know. I am sure."

"And my cousin Pinchas?"

"Pinchas and I were taken away together. But then, in one of the camps, we were separated and lost each other. But perhaps God was merciful and he was spared. And perhaps some of the other members of our family also."

Mordecai seemed bereft of speech. What was there to say. But he had to speak. Like a child he craved reassurance.

73

"Will they come back?" he cried out. "Will we find them?" There was desperation in the voice, but it was also a terrible cry for hope.

"I don't know," said David Mantel.

"Why am I alive? Why are you alive? Why did we come back?"

"Because it was willed."

"Who willed it?"

A long pause. Then David Mantel said quietly, "The Almighty."

Mordecai gave him a long, ironic look. "Do you really believe that?"

"I must."

"The great cosmic jokester," said Mordecai. "Do you really believe that he sits there in his heaven and plays a cruel game of chance with us? All a part of a great cosmic lottery?"

"It isn't for us to judge."

Mordecai raised himself on the bed and said angrily, "It is absolutely for us to judge. Who else can judge? Where did he hide during the great slaughter? Where was he, that almighty of yours? Where was he when we cried out to him?"

"I know all the questions. I have often asked them. But in the end I cannot judge Him. His ways are not our ways."

"No. That's not enough any more. If he is really there, he must answer. He must."

"There are signs of His Presence."

"There are more signs of his absence." Talking and concentrating had exhausted him. He let his head sink back into the pillow and closed his eyes.

After a while he heard footsteps out in the hallway, and then there was a knock on the door.

"That must be Rachel," said David Mantel. He rose to go to the door. "She has been here every day since you came."

"Rachel?"

"Yes. She came on the first morning to ask for you. But you were delirious. She said she met you the evening before,

74

and told you where you could find me. Don't you remember?"

Mordecai tried to recall the events of that day. There was a peasant. He remembered that. Gargoyles laughed at him. There was rubble. And then there was a woman in a dark street. He remembered that also. "I think I remember," he said. "But I don't know what she looked like."

There was another timid knock on the door.

"She's a pleasant woman," said David Mantel, and went to open the door.

"How is he?" Mordecai heard her ask with apprehension in the voice.

"He is awake. He has come back to us."

When she came into the room and he saw her, he remembered the gaunt face. Only now, in the daylight, it seemed a strangely beautiful face, with dark eyes glowing and the dark-brown hair pulled into a tight knot. She looked younger that he thought he remembered her, perhaps in her late twenties.

She smiled at him and without saying anything she sat down at the foot of the bed.

"She sat with you for hours every day," said David Mantel. "She nursed you. And when I thought you might leave us, she would not give up hope, and so she gave me courage, too."

"I must thank you, then," said Mordecai, and held out his hand.

She took his hand. "You don't owe me anything," she said softly. "I was glad I could help." She put her hand on his forehead and then stroked his face, heavy with several days' growth of beard. "Your fever is almost gone," she said.

He nodded. He took her hand and held it for a long time. A warm feeling suffused him. He felt very tired, drained of energy, but also, for the first time in many months, curiously at peace.

He closed his eyes and felt himself dozing off. When he woke again, she was still there, watching over him, but David

75

Mantel had left the room.

"You slept," she said.

"I didn't realize it," he answered. "How long have I been sleeping?"

"Over an hour. How do you feel?"

"Still tired. But much better. I think I will recover. I'm sure of it now."

"I always knew you would recover," she said.

"And will you stop coming now?"

"No, no," she said. "I'll come again....If you want me to," she added quickly.

"Oh, yes. I want you to come....You cared for me, even though I was a total stranger....I'm all alone in the world. I came home and found no one. Except my uncle. But all the others...."

"I'm also alone," she said.

"Come back, then. And then you and I will be less alone."

He held out his arms. She came close to him and he put his arms around her and drew her down and kissed her.

"As soon as I'm well again," he said after a while, "I'll have to leave this place."

"Where will you go?"

"I don't know. Except that I have to leave Europe. Europe is finished for me. I'll find some place. So long as it's far away. Where one can breathe. Where there isn't the stench of death everywhere."

"Yes."

"And you? What will you do?"

"I don't know. I — I have no plans. I live from day to day. I was pleased that I could come here and — and help you."

"Well, then, when I leave, perhaps you could come with me."

She was taken aback. "No, no," she cried. "How could I go with you? We don't even know each other."

"At least we're alive," he said. "We survived. And you

76

looked after me. That's already something."

"Perhaps it's something. But it may be nothing."

"We'll see."

"We'll see," she echoed him. "One day at a time."

"But you will come again?"

"Oh, yes. Yes, I'll come again. As long as you want me to come."

"Tomorrow?"

"Yes."

"And the day after."

"Yes."

"And the day after that?"

"I'm not yet ready to look so far into the future." She smiled, but it was an enigmatic smile.

"Are you serious?"

"Of course. I've been hurt too often. So I have to learn to trust again, and to hope again. One day at a time."

"All right," he said. "One day at a time." He stroked her face softly, and then drew her down and kissed her again.

"I must go now," she said. "And I'll come again tomorrow."

When she had gone, he lay for a long time without moving. He could still feel the warmth of her body. Perhaps I can pick up the pieces of my life, he thought. Perhaps I can find some reason to want to live again. The thought took him by surprise. It astonished him. It was miraculous how powerfully the will to live asserted itself.

He got out of bed. He felt weak and his legs were unsteady. He had to hold on to a chair. But he stood. His strength would return. And he knew that he would not allow himself to be defeated.

Annerl

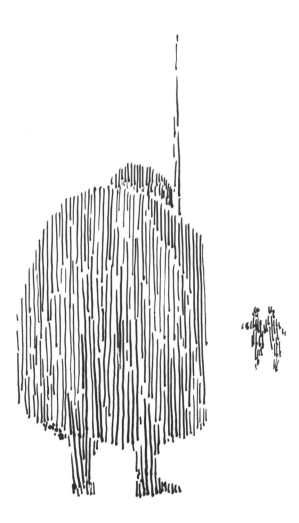

Annerl

We used to see her every day for four months of the year.
From the middle of November to the middle of March. When
the snow went from the streets of Vienna, Annerl went too.
During the warm season she was one of the host of women who
walked the streets in the morning, filling them with a familiar,
mournful cry. "Buuuy lavender! Freeesh lavender! Twenty
Groschen for a bushel of freeesh lavender! Buuuy lavender!" In
the afternoons she sold little packages of caraway seeds in the
market squares of the city. For four months of the year she sold
roasted chestnuts and baked potatoes on a corner which my
friend Heller and I had to pass on our way home from school.

She always hailed us when she saw us coming from afar.
"Heinrich! Heinrich! Mir graut's vor dir!" she would shout in
her raspy market-voice that had the mournful tinge of the
lavender women. "Heinrich! Heinrich! You disgust me!" and
then she would break into a soft, cackling laughter.

She could never remember Heller's name, or if she did
remember it, she never used it. To her he was always "you little
freckle-faced bastard", to which Heller would reply, his face
very stern, and his lips puckered up slightly, that his parents
had been married in church, and if she didn't believe it he would

bring a picture of his mother all in white, with a beautiful silken veil, "and two little boys went behind her," he said, "and carried the veil so it wouldn't drag on the floor and get all dirty." His voice became very solemn on these occasions, and Annerl would cackle a bit and say, "I know, I know. I don't mean it that way. Come 'ere, there's a chestnut for you, and now let's see you eat it, you little freckle-faced bastard. It's all in good faith, boy!"

Around the tenth of November, when the cold set in and we were beginning to wear our winter coats, we would start looking for her. Sometimes she didn't show up until the twentieth, but never later than that. We could see the big, grayish-black market umbrella, patched up with pieces of yellow and blue cloth, from a long way off.

"Annerl's back," I would say, prodding Heller in the ribs, and then we would start running. She always seemed glad to see us. She asked us what we'd done in the summer, and how we were getting along in school, and then came the inevitable conclusion. "You're growing up, lads. My, you're growing up. Bigger an' bigger every year. Just you keep growing like that, and you'll grow into heaven yet. You must be pretty near twelve."

"Thirteen," I said proudly. "I was thirteen last June, and Heller here was thirteen in October."

"Thirteen!" she exclaimed. "Thirteen! Why, you'd never believe that. Thirteen! You'll soon be going with the girls, and kissing them in the dark corners and doing things to them in the summer when the grass is high and soft." She laughed her dry, cackling laugh, fetching it deep from her chest, and she laughed still harder when she saw us blush crimson, for we had only recently been initiated into matters of sex and were still rather touchy on that point.

Annerl always looked the same. She never changed, and while she didn't grow younger, she didn't seem to grow any older either. She was a big woman, and her large buskins, coming up almost to her knees, and the thick, heavy clothes she wore, made her seem even bigger than she was. She was muffled in several sweaters, all of different colours, and on top of everything she wore a tremendous black overcoat, frayed around the edges and ripped and torn in several places. "I got that coat cheap," she remarked, "Bought it second-hand off a man. He bought it second-hand off another man. Made for a big man, all right. Made for a hell of a big man. But it keeps me warm when the wind is blowing hard around that corner."

Her face was earthen-coloured, a dirty, grayish-brown, with a vast network of wrinkles stretched across it that gave it a wizened appearance and made it look crude, as if a sculptor had hewn it roughly out of wood. She had a large, fleshy nose and a reddish wart right on top of it. I never saw her hair, because she always had it tucked tightly under a kerchief. She wore fingerless gloves on her big hands, and her fingers were very red, chapped by the cold, and her nails were broken and dirty.

She always sat on a little camp-stool. In front of her was the round, black brazier, with the chestnuts neatly placed around the rim and the baked potatoes piled in the middle. In the charcoal embers more chestnuts were roasting, and when they were ready she withdrew them with a pair of tongs and laid them around the rim. Behind her stood a big, wooden box in which she kept her provisions. The top of the box was always open to shield her from the draft, and arching above her was the grayish-black umbrella.

"The fellow that sold me that umbrella cheated me," she told us once. "Just let me lay my hands on him. I'm going to drag 'im here by his ears and knock that goddamn umbrella over his head till it cracks that brain o' his. 'Not a drop of rain'll ever get through that,' he told me. 'Not a drop,' he said. 'Best watertight umbrella money can buy,' he said. Look at it! Just you look at it! The rain and the snow leaking through it like it was a drainpipe, and me sitting here under it, catching the drops on my head."

Sometimes in the afternoons Josef, her husband, pottered about the stand. She called him Pepi, and she was always cursing him. He was a small old man, his face red and sodden from drink. "Thirty years now we been living together, an' he's never done an honest day's work in all the years," she used to say bitterly. "If he hasn't done it yet, he'll never do it now. Just eating an' sleeping an' drinking. That's all he ever done, but never done nothing to earn it. He's been living off me, sucking me dry for all them years, and beating me up in the nights when he comes home stinking with the drink. That's you I'm talking about, you, you miserable old dog. You never been good for nothing. Now go on, get me that bag of potatoes, and don't you run off with the money like you done last time."

And old Josef, very meek without his drink, cowering like a beaten dog, his overcoat held together by a piece of string, and his battered hat pushed deep into his face, would slink off to get the bag of potatoes. Sometimes Annerl asked us to go along with him and see that he didn't run off with the money to buy liquor.

"Don't you ever get mixed up with women," he warned us. "Stay away from sin. A woman is the curse of a man, leading him on into temptation. God have mercy on my soul." He crossed himself hurriedly. He became more eloquent as he panted along with the bag weighing heavy on his back. "See how mean she's to me. Making me work like I was a horse, and me weak in the bones and shaky all over."

They had had several children, but Annerl didn't know much about them. "Some of them died when I had 'em, and some died when they was babies sucking on the breast, and some of 'em growed up and left this city, and perhaps they even got out of the country, and some, they're still around somewhere, but I don't know where, and they never comes around to see me."

One day, towards the end of February, Annerl wasn't there. The wooden box was locked, the closed umbrella strapped tightly on top, and the round black brazier chained to a lamp-post. The windswept corner seemed like a desert without her. On the first day we remained loyal to Annerl, and walked home without stopping to buy chestnuts anywhere else.

"Let's save our money," said Heller, "and when she comes back we can buy twice as much."

She didn't come back tomorrow, nor the next day, and our loyalty didn't hold out that long. Temptation in the form of golden-brown chestnuts lay sprinkled too thick along the way, and going home without stopping off at some corner to eat a baked potato or some chestnuts somehow spoiled the rest of the day.

On the fourth day we could see her umbrella, and the yellow and blue patches of cloth.

"Annerl's back," I said. "She must have been sick."

She looked fine, and there was no change in her. Her voice was raspy and loud as always, and she cackled merrily when she saw us. We took our satchels from our backs and put them down on the ground.

"We missed you, Annerl," I said. "Where've you been? Were you sick in bed?"

"Sick?" she said, cackling softly, "he-he-he-he-he. Me sick? I don't get sick. I been standing on this corner for twenty-five years and more perhaps, in the rain and in the frost and in the snow, and I've not been sick a day. I don't aim to get sick. When my time's up, I just aim to die. I been away because Josef, that miserable, good-for-nothing old dog, just went and died on me."

We stared at her. Heller bowed his head and stopped munching his chestnut.

"Don't you go looking at me like that," she said. "I didn't kill him, though God knows many's the time that I could've chopped his head off like he was a chicken or a pig. But he just went and died on me quicker'n you can snap your fingers, and me hoping all the time that I would die first and leave 'im behind to look out for himself, and me praying every night that the good Lord would take me first. So what does He do? He goes and takes that dog first. It almost makes you think the Lord God don't hear no prayers any more." She crossed herself three times.

"The Lord God hears all our prayers," said Heller pompously. "He does not always choose to grant fulfilment."

"I don't know nothing 'bout that," snapped Annerl. "All I know is that I been hoping to get there first and look down on that miserable old dog, and see what he does when there's nobody to push the food down in his mouth, and nobody to pay the rent so he can have a bed to rest himself when he comes home stinking with the drink. So he goes and dies on me. Only two days before, he comes in at four in the morning, staggering and swaying round the room like he always done, and then fell in the bed and started beating his fists in my face like he was mad."

"Did he do that?" I asked. "Did he really do that?"

"He never knew what he was doing when he was crazy with the drink," she said. "Good thing he was so small an' I could handle him. I just pushed 'im right out and he fell on the floor and rolled 'imself up at the foot of the bed and there went to sleep, snoring his head off." She paused and wiped her nose, and there was a touch of tenderness in her voice when she said, "He was a right good 'un, he was, always wanting to make love, and by Jesus Christ, he could still do it when he was sober 'nough to know what the hell he was doing."

I leaned forward a bit and whispered confidentially, "How does a man do it when he makes love, Annerl?"

Heller leaned forward too.

Annerl laughed. "Never you mind how they do it, boys. Never you mind. You'll know soon enough how they do it when you do it." She turned to me. "You been eating five chestnuts," she said. "That's the sixth you're taking now. You never got more money than's enough to pay for two."

"I've got money today," I said. "I've got enough money to buy ten chestnuts today if I want to."

"What happened?" she said. "Your father robbed a bank or something?"

"No," I said, "I've got some money saved up."

86

"Let's see your money," she demanded.

I showed it to her.

She nodded her head. "It's going to snow this afternoon," she said, looking at the sky. "It's going to come down heavy this afternoon. Of all the times in the year he's got to pick the winter to die in, when the snow lies heavy on the graves and you can't put flowers on or nothing. I bought a wreath of evergreen and put it on the grave, but when the snow comes down heavy this afternoon it'll all be covered up. When I die now, there'll be no one left to put flowers on my grave, an' I always wished for a nice wreath o' carnations. They smell so sweet."

She stood up from her little stool and took a bag of charcoal from the box. She stirred the embers and the sparks came flying high from the brazier. Then she put more coals on. "My God," she said, looking into the slowly-glimmering fire, "unless his patron saint, the holy Josef, went up to the Lord to pray for him, he's surely gone to hell." She crossed herself. "I'm not wishing him any bad," she said quickly, looking at Heller who was gazing sternly at her. "I've done all I could for him. He's had a decent Christian burial, an' I bought two big candles and lit 'em in the church for 'im, and yesterday afternoon I went up to Father Berthold and paid good money so they would say a mass for 'im, and two monks are praying for his soul."

We had now finished our chestnuts and pulled out our money to pay her. She stretched out her hand to take it, hesitated, and then suddenly withdrew it.

"Ne'er mind the money today," she said. "Put it away. Go on, put it away, I said." She was almost shouting at us. "I don't want your money today."

We looked at each other, not knowing quite what to say.

"Wait a minute," she said, when we were finally turning to go. "Here." She picked up two baked potatoes, split them in the middle, put salt on them, and handed them to us. "Here," she said, "eat this on your way home, and never mind about the pay. He didn't have no wake or nothing, for there was no one cared for him. He was just a drunken, miserable old dog. Here, you take this an' eat it an' pray for his soul."

We took the potatoes, and Heller said, "Thank you, Annerl. We'll surely pray for his soul."

Then we picked up our satchels, slung them across our shoulders, and walked away slowly.

An Anonymous Letter

An Anonymous Letter

A sudden commotion woke the boy. He sat up in bed and listened half-asleep to the raised voices of his mother and father. They were quarrelling. The boy tried to make out their words, but he couldn't, and so he got up and groped his way out of the dark bedroom, and when he opened the door and stood in the hall their voices seemed shriller and uglier than before. His parents had often quarrelled, but their quarrels had never been so violent before. As he came closer to the living-room, he felt his heart beating and he was afraid.

His parents stopped shouting at each other as soon as they saw him, and a brooding, dangerous silence seemed to settle over the room and was almost worse than the tangible voices. The strong light in the room hurt the boy's eyes and he closed them for a moment and everything was red and yellow. He rubbed his eyes with his fingers, feeling wide awake and yet sleepy. That was a curious feeling.

"David!" he heard his father say. "Why did you get up!"

The boy opened his eyes, and became suddenly aware that his father was fully dressed. He had his glasses on, and he wore a dark gray, striped suit and a red tie, and his hair was neatly combed. So he couldn't have been in bed yet, the boy

91

thought. He must have just come in a little while ago. It must be very late. Was that why they were quarrelling so violently?

"I woke up because of the noise you and Mom made," said the boy quietly.

He moved his eyes slowly away from his father and looked now closely at his mother. She was standing there in her dressing-gown. In her hand she held a large, crumpled piece of yellow paper. Her hair was dishevelled. Loose locks seemed to be sticking out all over, like pieces of thick string. Her face looked very pale without any rouge or lipstick. She looked pretty awful, the boy thought, gazing down at the floor. Not like the glamorous women in the movies. They were always sleek and beautiful, with their hair curling and their lips fresh, even when they'd just got out of bed. He knew deep down that people never really looked so lovely when they got out of bed, he knew he looked pretty awful in his wrinkled-up pyjamas, with his hair all mussed. But his mother could look pretty nice sometimes, when her hair was all set and combed and her face made up, and when she wore a sleek-fitting dress and high-heeled shoes and nylon stockings. But now she didn't look very nice, and he wished he didn't have to look at her.

"What happened?" he asked. "Why are you shouting at each other?"

"Because your mother believes everything, just so long as it's written down," said his father.

"Ask your father where he was until nearly three in the morning."

"I told you," said his father calmly. "I was playing poker over at Eddie's place. It got late. That's all there is to it."

"Was *she* there, too?" asked his mother. Her hand closed tightly around the piece of yellow paper, and the boy saw that she was trembling.

"Rubbish!" his father cried. His face was red, and blue veins began to show on his temples, but he was trying to control the rising anger, and said with elaborate irony, "Sure, sure. There was Eddie, and Arnold Griffin and Joe Holmes and—

and *she*, a beautiful, beautiful, slim blonde. And we were all playing poker together."

"Very funny," said his mother. "Very funny indeed. But it doesn't dispose of the letter. And you'd better explain it to me."

"Now listen," said his father, his voice rising in anger again. "That letter — it's — it's criminal libel, that's what it is. Whoever wrote it ought to be ashamed of themselves. Rubbish belongs in the garbage can, not in the living-room. You ought to know that."

"What letter are you talking about?" asked the boy. "Who wrote it?"

His mother suddenly thrust out the hand that clutched the yellow piece of paper, and said, "Here. Look at it and see for yourself."

"No," his father cried. "No. He's too young to see that kind of rubbish."

"He's old enough," said his mother. "Let him know about it."

The veins in his father's temples stood out more prominently than before, and he pulled his lower lip between his teeth. He looked piercingly at his son. The light from a lamp was reflected in his glasses and made his pupils look like two thin yellow points.

The boy looked down at the piece of paper his mother had handed him and began to smooth it out. On it there was a brief, clumsily written, unsigned note. "Dear Mrs. Wright," the boy read. "You will be interested to know that your husband is carrying on with another woman. They go out together and they come back to her apartment together. You will be interested to know this."

The boy read the letter twice. His eyes widened as he read it, and he felt a strange tingling all down his back, as if tiny mice were running up and down his spine. He handed the letter back to his mother and then stared down at the floor. His body began to shiver slightly, though he wasn't cold. Words seemed to form in his throat, but his throat seemed suddenly dry and he could make no sound. Neither his father nor his mother said anything and an oppressive silence settled down over the room like a cloud.

At last his father spoke. "So now you've done it," he said. "You've let him read that piece of dirt. And now what?"

"Nothing," said his mother defiantly. "Just let him know about it, so he can make up his own mind." Her voice trailed away, as if she were unsure of herself, as if she now regretted having let the boy see the letter.

"Make up his own mind!" his father taunted her. "About what? About an anonymous letter! About a piece of malicious . . . . Listen!" He turned to the boy and said almost savagely, "Somebody hasn't even the guts to sign their letter and your mother thinks it's the gospel truth."

"It isn't true, then?" the boy said, uncertain whether to believe what he had read or not. He distrusted tale-bearers. Whoever had written that letter was a rat, he thought, even if it was true.

"It's a lie," his father said. "It's a rotten lie. Let's hear no more about it. I'm sick of it all." He flung his left arm out violently, as if he were hurling something from him in disgust, and then he stalked out of the room abruptly. In the doorway he turned again and said mockingly, "Ask your mother why she doesn't have me followed if she's so sure."

His mother seemed to freeze where she stood. "Why," she said, "I—I wouldn't lower myself . . . ."

But he was already walking down the hall, into the bedroom, ignoring her.

The boy sat there, staring down at the floor, thinking, and when he glanced up he saw his mother's face looking drawn and desperate. She looked old suddenly, her hair now everywhere streaked with grey, and he felt a great pity for her.

"I'm sorry I showed you the letter, David," she said very softly. "I shouldn't have. You're too young to know about these things. But I just had to, so you'd know what I go through."

She walked over to the chesterfield and sat down beside

94

him.

"You don't have to believe it," he said. "It's not true, anyway. It's a lie."

"I wish I could believe that," she said. Her voice was flat and resigned. All the anger had gone out of it. "But it's true. I know it's true."

"How do you know?" he asked.

"I just know," she said. Silently, tears came and ran down her cheeks.

"But it's only a letter," he said. "And it's not even signed."

"Go to bed now," she said, stroking his hair. "You have to go to school tomorrow."

He wished she wouldn't remind him of school, for he felt very grown up suddenly. He saw the tears streaming down her face and he almost had to cry himself. But he didn't want to cry, and he jumped up impulsively and without saying any more ran back into his room, leaving her sitting there on the chesterfield, desolate and alone.

Sleep wouldn't come. As soon as he closed his eyes the room began to see-saw violently, and he opened his eyes again and sat up in bed because he felt he would be sick otherwise. So he sat brooding on the edge of his bed, his feet dangling down to the floor, and put his hands up to his head. There was a dull pain just behind his eyeballs, and when he pressed down on his eyes with his fingers, it got worse.

He had weak eyes, like his father. Sometimes, especially toward the end of the month, his father's eyes would be red and watery, and when he came home from the office he often bathed them with boracic acid. His father was an accountant and the end of the month was his busiest time, and he often went back to the office after supper to do some more work, and sometimes he didn't come home for supper at all, but stayed downtown.

Could the letter be true, the boy thought, opening his eyes and staring out into the dark room. Suddenly he became conscious of his alarm clock. Its ticking, jerky somehow, feverish almost, seemed to pound directly in his head, and he jumped up and grabbed the alarm clock from the dresser and buried it under his pillow.

What was true and what was false? Should he believe his mother or his father? Whoever had written that letter knew his mother's name. But that meant nothing. Somebody might have a grudge against her or against his father. But what if it was true? Carrying on with another woman. That's what the letter says, he thought. And when they came together to this woman's apartment, what happened then? What did they do there?

He had never thought of his father as romantic. His hair was turning gray and he wore glasses and his voice was often raspy. He had sometimes tried to imagine how his father and his mother looked when they were going steady, long before he was born, but he could never do it. There was a picture of his mother and his father that showed them on their wedding day, with his mother all in white, holding a bouquet of roses, and his father, without glasses and much slimmer than he was now, wearing an old-fashioned tail-coat, standing beside her. But the picture had never seemed quite real to him. It was just a yellowing photograph, and the couple in it might be any couple photographed together long, long ago.

But if there was really another woman, the boy thought, what did she look like? Was she young and beautiful? She'd have to be younger and more beautiful than his mother, he thought, or else why would his father bother with her? But if she was young and beautiful, why would she bother with his father? His father said it was all a lie, but his mother said it was true. Then who was right?

In school the next day he paid hardly any attention, and was reprimanded several times. He felt very tired and depressed, but at the same time also keyed up and tense, his mind in turmoil. The hours seemed endless, and when the noon bell finally rang it sounded more sweetly than he had ever heard it before, promising deliverance.

Outside the school he wondered whether he should wait

for his friend Tom, who was in another class. They lived on the same street and always walked home together. But before he could make up his mind, Tom joined him and they set off as usual. Tom began to talk about football, and they discussed their team's chances in next Saturday's game, but he couldn't get worked up about that today and suddenly he switched the subject.

"D'you remember the movie we saw about three weeks ago?" he asked.

"Which one?"

"I don't remember the name," he said, "but it was all about a man and his wife, and this man met another woman, and—well, they carried on together."

"Mhm," said Tom. "I remember. What about that movie?"

"Nothing. Except that—well, I dreamt about that picture last night, and—it sort of keeps bothering me."

"Why?"

"Because—well, I—I really don't know. Except . . . Say you get married and the girl you marry did that. You know. Carry—I mean go out with another man. But say you know nothing about it until somebody writes you a letter about it, but never signs his name."

"That's not how it was in the movie," his friend said.

"I know. But that's what I was thinking. Say it was like I was saying. What would you do?"

"I'd try to find out, naturally."

"But how?"

"Easy. I'd try and see her going out with that other man."

"And once you'd seen her?"

"I'd knock him cold," said Tom without hesitation and balled his left hand into a fist.

"And what would you do to her?"

The question seemed to stump Tom. He stopped walking and thought for a moment. "I might take her back if I was really in love with her, but if I wasn't any more I might just kick her

97

out."

He seemed satisfied with that solution, but David was no longer listening to him, for he suddenly knew what he must do.

When the long school day was finally over he rushed out of the building, and dashed across the street, where he caught a bus that took him straight downtown. In a drugstore exactly opposite the brick office building where his father worked he took up his vigil. He went over to the magazine racks and pretended to look at a magazine, but all the while his eyes never left the door of the building across the road. He persuaded himself that he was a detective following up some clues that might lead him to a world-shaking discovery of a great conspiracy, but he left the nature of the conspiracy deliberately vague. Desperately he tried to hide from himself the real reason why he was there, because he hated to think that he was snooping on his father. The school books he carried grew heavy and he kept shifting them from arm to arm. As the clock moved toward five, the flow of people from the building across the street increased, and the boy grew more excited and tense. At last his father came out, talking to another man, and they walked down the street together. The boy followed them at a distance. At the bus stop they parted. Then his father got on a number 6 bus, and the boy knew that he was going straight home.

Twice more he went downtown, driven by an impulse of which he was secretly ashamed, but twice more he merely saw his father catch a bus straight home.

The letter was not mentioned again. His mother and father seemed to have concluded a kind of truce, for while they did not talk much to each other, they did not quarrel either. Then one evening toward the end of the month his father remarked casually that the work was beginning to pile up and that he would stay at the office the next evening to try and clear things up.

As soon as school finished next day, the boy took a bus downtown, and after he had walked about for a while he went again into the large drugstore from which he could observe the building across the street. He stared straight out through the big plate-glass window, paying no attention to anything that was going on around him. There was a moment when he began to feel slightly ridiculous for having come at all. He no longer even pretended that he had come to make a great discovery. After a while his eyes strayed from the window and he noticed a big-hipped woman standing beside him, leafing through a magazine. When she turned the pages, he noticed that her long fingernails were painted bright red.

It was now nearly five o'clock and he began to look out for his father. At last he saw him coming out of the building, but he did not as usual walk toward the bus stop, but crossed the street and made directly for the drugstore. In consternation the boy moved toward the back of the store, trying to make himself as inconspicuous as possible amid the displays of lipsticks and hair-lotions. A clerk came up to him and asked him what he wanted, and he stammered something about chewing gum, keeping his head turned toward the back of the store and hoping his father wouldn't see him, so he wouldn't have to make up a story of why he was here. He paid for his chewing gum and then slowly, surreptitiously, he glanced around, and there was his father talking to the woman who'd stood beside him and whose red fingernails he had noticed. Now his father said something and they both laughed, and then his father walked over to one of the counters and bought some cigarettes. Then he went to the door, held it open for the woman, smiling at her, and they walked out of the store together, and together they went down the street.

By the time the boy came out of the store, his father and the woman had walked almost to the intersection at the end of the block, past the bus stop. Keeping his eyes on them, the boy followed them. The street was crowded, but to him it seemed as if nobody were walking there except this man and this woman, and he knew that he must not lose sight of them, but at the same time was forbidden to come close. It all seemed like a dream.

Everything was clear, and everything was also very hazy, and though he felt very calm, he was also in a strange way very excited. Somewhere far away he could hear the sound of motors, and once he knew he had bumped into somebody, for he heard a man's voice saying, "Look where you're going," but he paid no attention. So he walked blindly on, never losing sight of his father and that woman, threading his way automatically through the crowd that flowed up and down the street, until at last, after what seemed an eternity of walking, his father and the woman turned and went into a restaurant.

The boy stopped walking and began to think about what he should do. Slowly, stealthily almost, as if he were treading on forbidden ground, he walked up to the restaurant and stood on the pavement, silently pondering. From where he stood he could see the cashier's desk, and in the large window that gave upon the street there was a tank in which goldfish swam. Beyond it there moved the shadowy figures of men and women.

Was that the woman, he thought. But she was not beautiful. He could not really say what her face was like, but her figure was not very beautiful. She had large hips, and her legs were thick. He had observed them, though only from a distance. And she also had very long fingernails. They reminded him of claws. But if someone had told him, when this woman came into the drugstore, that she was the woman of the anonymous letter, he would not have believed it. He did not believe it yet. Not really deep down.

But if it was true, he thought, then his father had lied to him. This realization, he knew, ought to shock him, but it didn't. It was some time now since he had ceased to believe in the all-wisdom, the all-honesty, and the all-powerfulness of parents. He had sometimes lied himself, reluctantly, unwillingly, and a sense of guilt had clung to him often, but he had gotten over it in a few days. Almost everybody felt forced to tell lies now and then. He knew that, and he could forgive in others what he had done himself. But she was not beautiful— this woman. She was not worth lying about. To walk with her down the street was not romantic. His mother was much more beautiful. Much more. And he felt a sudden resentment, anger even, welling up within him because his father had inflicted pain on his mother for the sake of this woman who was not even beautiful. And suddenly he wanted to be his mother's defender, the fierce champion of her cause. But what could he do except gape on impotently?

All at once, without clearly knowing what he was going to do, he found himself walking, as if in his sleep, toward the door of the restaurant. He pushed the door open and stood inside. Past the arborite-topped counter and the little black swivel-stools, past two gleaming copper coffee urns, there was a half-open folding door. Beyond it was the dining-room, and he walked uncertainly toward it. A black-coated waiter was standing there with a large menu in his hand. Did he wish to have dinner in the dining-room?

"No," he answered, shaking his head. "I'm just looking for my father."

The waiter stepped aside, and the boy walked into a long, narrow dining-room, so dimly lit that it took him a moment to make out some of the objects. All the tables had deep-red tablecloths, and on each table there stood a tall, slender vase, holding a single flower. Soft music was piped into the dining-room and mingled with the discreet clatter of knives and forks. At first he didn't see his father, but then he saw him, and began to make his way to the table where they sat—his father and that woman. He walked very slowly, because he was afraid, and secretly ashamed too. He tried to think what he should say when he came face to face with his father, when suddenly he heard his father's voice crying out, "David!"

Surprise and astonishment were mingled in the voice, and it seemed to the boy as if his name were reverberating through the dining-room. Two or three people turned to look at him as he stood silently, unable to speak, and stared at his father, and then slowly let his eyes move to the woman, who was as petrified as he and stared back at him, a half-crumbled soda cracker in a hand which seemed to have been arrested in mid-air.

The hand had red fingernails. That was what he saw first. Then he became conscious of a huge red mouth that was half open, as if the jaws had locked. Only slowly did the rest of her features become distinguishable to him. Her face, heavily rouged and powdered, seemed puffy and soft-fleshed, and the boy thought that if he stretched out his hand and touched her face, it would feel like a sponge. She wore a necklace of small pearls, and the pearls glowed warm against her throat. The necklace was the only thing about the woman that he found at all attractive.

"How did you get here?" The fury in his father's voice was not disguised by his attempt to speak calmly.

"Who is he, anyway?" the woman asked. She put the soda cracker on a plate and looked at his father, clearly puzzled.

The boy meant to tell her who he was, but he couldn't say anything. He felt hopelessly inadequate, stumbling about in a dark and fearful forest.

"You must have followed us," his father said. "You must have actually followed us."

The boy winced when he heard his father say that. He didn't want to be a sneak, slinking furtively round corners.

A waiter brushed past him, saying impatiently, "Don't block the way, please."

"Don't stand in the way, son," his father said angrily.

The woman gasped and put her hand up to her mouth. "That's not your son?" she cried.

"Yes," his father said, "Yes, it is."

The boy sat down on the chair beside his father, wishing desperately that he could vanish somehow. He became aware of a heavy lavender perfume that seemed to float in the air above the table like a low cloud. He raised his eyes and saw her big, round bosom and quickly looked away again.

"I didn't know you had a son," she stammered. "That big. You never told me."

His father ignored her. "Your mother put you up to this," he said. "Snooping about like a dog. Didn't she?"

"No," the boy cried fiercely. "No. She had nothing to do with it." He contracted his eyebrows and glowered at the woman.

"I'm going," the woman cried suddenly. "I'm not going to sit here and have him stare at me like that. What does he think I am?"

"Don't," his father said hastily. "Don't."

But she was already on her feet, and with a violent toss of her head she turned and hurried out of the restaurant. His father rushed after her, but she disappeared and he came back to the table alone.

"You can go home now," he said acidly, "and tell your mother how you spied on me."

The boy didn't say anything. That was another matter he would have to think about. Whether to tell his mother. Everything was too tangled up and nothing could ever be simple and straightforward again. Somehow his father had managed to hit him where he felt most vulnerable. He despised himself for having spied. There was something mean about his action. But his father had no moral right to hold it against him.

He fixed his eyes upon his father. "Is that the woman you—carry on with?" he said and stopped. He could hardly get the words out. They seemed to stick in his throat. "She looks awful," he cried viciously. "Just awful."

He knew at once, by the way his father winced and turned his eyes away, that this remark had hurt him more than if someone had thrown a stone at him.

The Travelling Nude

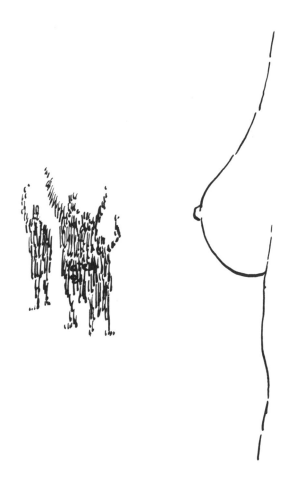

The Travelling Nude

I

The only thing about the whole affair that worries me a bit is how I am going to explain to my father why I threw up a good job. My father is a very unimaginative man, and I know he has been brooding about me for a long time. Now when he hears about the travelling nude, he's quite likely to become momentarily deranged. But that, I'm afraid, can't be helped.

Ever since the subject was first broached and the debate got passionate, splitting at least one husband and wife right down the middle, I've had a very distinct impression of her. I admit it's ludicrous, but you'll admit (though my father isn't likely to) that it has a certain kind of charm.

There she is. Quite good-looking. Not anything spectacular, you understand. The pay is hardly good enough to attract anything like that, and the conditions of work are not exactly first class. There's a lot of travelling involved, and the work has to be done mostly in small towns, pop. 1275 or 1423, and she has to stay in rather dingy hotels, even though these hotels have fancy names, like the *Ritz* or the *Imperial*. But she has a pretty good figure, nonetheless. Nicely proportioned. Breasts pretty firm, though perhaps now beginning to droop a little, with the first flush of youth departed. A bit of a fatty fold starting to show round her middle. But the buttocks still firm, and the thighs round and full, and the legs long and shapely. A good nude, take it all in all. Now she goes to all these little places, pop. 1500 and less, a different place each week, and wherever she goes (my father is going to find this hard to understand) she travels in the nude. She wears nothing except a pair of high-heeled shoes. Even in the winter when it's very cold. She's a travelling nude, you see. And she travels out of Edmonton, Alberta, pop. 250,000 or so, a fair-sized city.

She takes a taxi from the house she rooms in (that's part of allowable expenses) to either the C.P.R. or C.N.R. or the Greyhound Bus Station, and there she gets out, proud, head held high, but she's very demure and a bit shy at the same time. So with a nonchalantly grand manner she tips the taxi driver ten cents and walks into the station. He's a bit pop-eyed, and so are most of the other people, but I never worry very much about their reaction. She's accepted, more or less. She's known as the travelling nude and that's all there is to it.

Sometimes, in the winter, I feel I'd like to drape a warm coat around her, but I resist the impulse. She's a hardy soul. She can stand the cold. Anyway, there she goes. Oh, I forgot to tell you. She also carries a handbag. She is, after all, a woman. So she traipses up to the ticket window, and says (her voice is husky, in a feminine, though not exactly seductive way), "One ticket, return, to Great Fish Lake, please." Or it might be Three Bear Hills, or Pollux, or Castor, or any number of other places, for she is constantly kept busy for eight or nine months of the year. And then she rummages about in her capacious handbag, pays for her ticket, looks somewhat disapprovingly at the astonished clerk who gapes wide-eyed at her slightly drooping breasts (the first flush of youth now gone), not knowing whether to be scandalized or erotically aroused, and then walks over to the news-stand and buys, as is her custom, a copy of the *Ladies' Home Journal* or *Chatelaine* or *Vogue*, for she must know what the well-dressed woman wears this season, or what Dr. Blatz or Dr. Spock thinks this month about the psyche of

108

the pre-school child, or what delicious dishes can be concocted this week out of last Sunday's left-over roast. She is a well-informed nude, you see, garnering up bits of useful information as she travels by train or bus.

So she arrives at last in Great Fish Lake, or Three Bear Hills, or Castor, or Pollux, and gets off the bus or the train, and the station-master and the local inhabitants look at each other knowingly and say, "Oh, here goes the travelling nude. Guess there's going to be a great deal of activity over at the Community Hall tonight," and they smile and wink broadly at each other, but look very soberly as she walks past them, and doff their hats and say, "Good afternoon, Ma'm. Not too cold for you, I hope," and she smiles back graciously, showing as she does so a gap (unfortunate blemish!) in the upper row of her teeth.

And the desk-clerk at the *Great Fish Lake Imperial* or the *Three Bear Hills Ritz*, wooden buildings, once painted white, with name emblazoned in black block letters, looks down the main street and sees her coming, and says to a man drowsing in a sagging, brown, cracked leather chair, "There's the travelling nude. That means the old Community Hall is going to be all lit up tonight," and winks at the man in the sagging chair, who rouses himself with a startled snore and looks at her as she walks towards the hotel, balancing delicately on her high-heeled shoes, her handbag now slung across her shoulder.

The desk-clerk has her key ready. "Same room as last time, Ma'm. 14A." The number 13 is delicately skipped at the *Great Fish Lake Imperial* or the *Three Bear Hills Ritz*.

She smiles her gap-toothed smile, thanks him, and taking her key, walks up the stairs, and the two men look thoughtfully at her firm buttocks swaying lightly from side to side as she mounts to the first floor and lets herself into her room.

Once in, she sighs deeply and lies down on her bed. A long evening's work now stretches before her, and she does not anticipate it with particular pleasure. The work is tiring, and she feels tired already, even before it's begun, for she's no longer

109

quite as energetic as she once was.

Evening comes. A few street lights in the main street go on, and the gray-haired, mustachioed caretaker gets everything ready, and then, singly or in groups, they begin to emerge from the small houses in the unlit streets or from farmhouses further away, making their way on foot or in cars that bump along rutty roads, and so at last converge upon the Community Hall, and, carrying satchels and sundry other equipment, greet each other and go into the Hall and sit down busily on chairs arranged in a wide semi-circle, and now, talking to each other, they wait. There are pinched-looking women, resigned to spinsterhood, and middle-aged matrons, their child-rearing task now done; there are a few youngish couples, and two or three single men.

"Are we all here?" says a cheerful female voice. "Good. Now we must really work tonight. She'll be here in a minute. Take advantage of your opportunity. Remember, she won't be here for another six months or so."

Out of the satchels come sheets of drawing paper and charcoal pencils, and they all sit there, poised, expectant, ready for action.

The door opens and with stately steps, head held high, her bearing almost regal, the travelling nude enters, making her way smiling, as if bestowing royal grace, to a chair in the middle of the semi-circle and sits down. Her work has now begun.

"Now, class," says the cheerful female, who teaches in the local elementary school during the day, "tonight we'll try and draw the sitting nude. Tomorrow we'll draw the nude standing, and the day after that the reclining nude. I hope you'll all be here again then, for as Mr. Mahler told us, we cannot become painters without learning to draw the human figure exactly, can we now?" And smiles all round the semi-circle, and then nods pleasantly at the sitting travelling nude.

The travelling nude arranges herself on her chair, trying to make herself as comfortable as possible. She now seems oblivious of the faces staring at her. Each face now sees her from its own angle. There is a pause while each drinks in the vision of "Figure. Female. Sitting. Nude." At last they begin to sketch away, now satisfied, now frustrated; erase, start again; look over their shoulders to see what their neighbors are doing, while all the while the cheerful female circulates among them, admonishing, guiding, calling on the team to give their all. "Be sure and remember that Mr. Mahler comes next month," she cries, "and that we want to show him that we've really been making progress."

So for three evenings they sketch the travelling nude until their creative energies are quite exhausted, their paper all used up, their pencils blunt.

Early in the morning, on the fourth day after her arrival, the travelling nude departs. She is glad the work for this week is over, looks forward to lounging about for a few days in Edmonton. She is quite tired, for the accommodation is dingy, the food stale and steamy, and the work is strenuous, exhausting even. And yet she knows that in the following week she will set out again and spend three days in some little town to help along the growth of culture in the land.

II

Perhaps it would be better if I made up some commonplace story and never said anything at all about the travelling nude to my father. For if I told him the truth, I would only succeed in calling forth his Job-like posture. On such occasions he sighs deeply, lifts his head toward the ceiling of the room, as if God sat there in a corner, rolls his eyes, and spreads his arms out wide, resigned to his martyrdom. "Everybody has some cross to bear," he told me once. "You are my cross." I'm sure he thinks I am mad.

It occurs to me that you might think so, too. Let me assure you that I am as sane as you. I am an artist. My name is

Herman O. Mahler. I am aware that "Mahler" is the German word for painter. So perhaps long ago one of my ancestors was a painter, and the thought that this familial talent, after lying dormant for many generations, burst forth again and manifested itself in me, makes me quite excited, creating a bond between me and that remote ancestor whose name proclaimed his art. My father sneered at the notion. So far as he knew or cared to admit the Mahlers were all respectable businessmen, ever since the first Canadian Mahler, my grandfather, established a general store in Orillia, a small Ontario town. I myself was born in Toronto twenty-seven years ago.

When I announced my intention of becoming a painter, my father stormed up and down our living room, crying incessantly, "Why did I slave all these years? For what? For what? What was the point? What?"

I, for my part, kept on saying, "I don't see any logical connection here," but he merely repeated, "Why did I slave all these years? For what? For what?"

My mother didn't take any of this seriously. She thought my ambition would burn itself out. I was only seventeen at the time. But when the flames burned ever lustier, my mother, who is a realistic woman, persuaded my father to let me go to the Ontario College of Art.

He looked the place over and was quite impressed by its size and general air of stolidity. As he put it to my mother, "The building is beautiful. Big solid pillars. Good stone. Nice trees all around. And the inside, too. Respectable. Quiet. Clean. Not like those attics you hear about. Well, maybe there's something to this art business after all."

I studied at the Ontario College of Art for three years, learned to draw "Figure. Female. Reclining. Nude." "Figure. Female. Sitting. Nude." Learned to work in oil, tempera, and various other media, took several courses in the history of art, and emerged at last a duly certified Mahler.

By the time I was twenty-four or twenty-five I had already passed through several well-recognizable periods. My first period was the blue period, and it is astonishing what nuances of blue I could produce. My style then was generally realistic, although my father, on seeing one of my paintings, exclaimed, "Blue horses! Why, that's impossible! Who ever saw a blue horse?"

I moved on to my pink period and painted in pink more or less the same subjects which I had hitherto painted in blue. "Pink horses!" my father exclaimed. "Why, that's impossible! Who ever saw a pink horse?"

I moved rapidly on to my Cubist period, in which I produced at least one remarkable painting, a largish oil, entitled, "Nude Descending Staircase," which practically caused my father to suffer an apoplexy and to mutter darkly about fraud and the corruption of the young. It was the title that annoyed him, for he could recognize no nude in the picture itself. My mother contented herself with a clicking of her tongue and a modest statement that these things were beyond her.

After my Cubist period came my Abstract period, and at last I felt that I had found my style. Here imagination was not restricted. I felt free, with all nature at my feet. I was a conqueror. Neither space nor time could now contain me. My father was now quite certain that I was mad.

In five years of painting I sold paintings totalling two hundred dollars, and even my poor mathematical brain managed to compute that this amounted to only forty dollars per annum. What was most irksome, however, was the fact that since I continued to live at home and was therefore in a manner of speaking a kept man, my father, who was after all doing the keeping, felt himself entitled to keep up a consistent, sniping, carping sort of criticism about the noble art of painting in general and my own activity in particular. He wondered why this curse had been wished on his only son, for whom he had envisaged a bright and rosy future in the retailing business. The idea that I was carrying on the tradition established by a remote Mahler he dismissed with contempt.

113

At last he began to insist that I earn my own living. What was I to do? I refused to prostitute my original, God-given talent, for I felt that if I did so I would in some obscure way be betraying the honour and integrity of that remote Mahler who had passed on his mantle to me and was now watching to see what I would do with it. Imagine my joy, therefore, when I read in an art magazine that the Extension Department of the University of Alberta was looking for an Extension lecturer in art, whose business it would be to travel the length and breadth of the province and give a series of short courses (none longer than a week) in various small towns. What marvellous vistas opened up before me! I would be a true servant of the noble art of painting. What hidden talents I would discover, what rough diamonds I would unearth, polish and present to the world! And I would go on painting myself. Thus I could pursue the noble art to which I had dedicated myself and keep on eating at the same time without relying on the charity of my father or prostituting the inner me.

I applied for the job and was duly appointed.

III

I resigned from this position largely because of the travelling nude.

I must be frank. The rough diamonds I hoped to find turned out to be chunks of coal. And not even coal of the first grade, either. But they were most pleasant pieces of coal, kind and most appreciative. I became known in the little towns and in the pokey hotels, and held forth in sundry Community Halls on the elements of the noble art of painting as taught in the Ontario College of Art. Thus is the light spread into the furthermost corners of the land.

Most of my students were unfortunately wholly intent on reproducing mountains and lakes and flowers with a passion

114

that depressed me. "More imagination!" I cried. "Use all the imagination you have!" Whereupon dear Mrs. McGregor, when next I arrived in her neck of the woods, showed proudly a canvas on which she had painted a desert sheik, in long white robes and red fez, sitting in a posture meant to be majestic on an improbable-looking Arabian horse, and staring at what was unquestionably a frozen lake in front of him, and the snow-capped Rocky Mountains ringing him all round. The critical mind stood awed and aghast. All I could mutter was, "You could improve the folds in the sheik's robe."

I did not despair. My earnest hope was to guide my charges away from nature and lead them, via the human figure, to the glory and perfect freedom of Abstraction. I began first by having one or another of my students pose, and I showed them how a face could be broken down into its geometrical components. It was rather more difficult to demonstrate how the clothed body could be broken down, and it was in Three Bear Hills that I made the fatal remark.

"What we need for a real study of the human figure," I said, "is someone to model for us in the nude."

Well, the ice descended on the Three Bear Hills Community Hall. Shocked looks crissed and crossed, and dear Mrs. McGregor looked at me with infinite pain, as if to say, "You wouldn't surely mean me?"

I found myself shaking my head and mumbling, "No. No. That is not what I meant at all," when suddenly there was the unmistakable gravel voice of Thomas Cullen breaking the icy silence with a loud "Hear! Hear!"

I turned to look at him, and there he was, as sprightly a sixty-year-old as ever you saw, small and wiry, with a little bald-pated head, looking straight at Nancy Hall, a fair to middling thirty-year-old blossoming bud, and "Hear! Hear!" he cried again. "That's what we need all right."

"Shame!" cried dear Mrs. McGregor. "Shame!"

"For academic purposes merely," said Thomas Cullen saucily.

"Shame!" cried Mrs. McGregor again. "Shame!"

I managed to smooth things over, but the fertile seed continued to sprout in Thomas Cullen's bald-pated head and the following June bore glorious fruit in Medicine Hat.

Once a year there is a meeting of the Community Art Classes in one of the larger centres, and whoever has the time gathers there for a shindig lasting a day. There are discussions in small groups about how things could be improved and then all the students exhibit their pictures, and in the evening there's a banquet and there's a guest speaker, and afterwards the group chairmen present a series of resolutions and everybody votes on them, and then, in a softly-glowing mood of togetherness and comradeship the group dissolves, thinking that the art of painting has been truly and nobly served.

As leader and travelling mentor I was expected to arrange this annual event, and things went pretty smoothly. That ancient Mahler might have thought the guild of medieval painters had been miraculously revived, until, of course, he'd seen the paintings. After the discussions and the exhibition we all gathered in the banqueting room of a restaurant, and sat on hard, narrow chairs around long tables, eating tough chicken and soggy boiled potatoes and dried-out cole slaw. After the dessert, I rapped a teaspoon against a glass and introduced our guest speaker, a nice enough fellow who'd come out of Edmonton at my request, and who now began to warble about the aesthetics of modern art, and threw names about, like Leger, and Braque, and Mondrian, and Picasso, and everybody nodded knowingly, feeling cultured and really dead centre, if you know what I mean. At last he finished warbling and sat down amid polite applause.

The next item on the agenda was "Resolutions." It's funny, but I can never even think of the word "resolution" without at once seeing a wastepaper basket. I guess that is what Freud meant by free association. A procession of wastepaper baskets now began to march through my head as our little band of devotees resolved in various ways to make the cultural desert

116

bloom.

It was getting pretty hot and my chair seemed to be getting smaller and smaller, and just as I thought we were all done, there was the loud clearing of a throat, and Thomas Cullen cried out, "I have another resolution, Mr. Chairman."

Another wastepaper basket strutted slowly through my head. "But," I said, "you didn't chair one of the groups, did you, Mr. Cullen?"

"No," said Thomas Cullen, "I did not. This is a private resolution." He cleared his throat again and took a sip of water. Then he got up, straightened his tie, reached deep into the inner recesses of his breast-pocket and brought out a piece of paper.

"Inasmuch and because no painter can call himself a painter unless he knows the anatomy of the human figure," Thomas Cullen read solemnly, "and inasmuch as it is impossible to study and know the human figure unless that figure is nude, be it therefore resolved that the authorities in question secure a travelling nude who would go from community to community . . . ."

Thomas Cullen had more to say, but I didn't hear it. For, like Venus rising from the waves, the travelling nude rose in my mind, fully fashioned, although with the first flush of youth now gone.

The next voice I heard distinctly was that of Mr. Edward Nash, who sat next to his wife, and who now said loudly and clearly, "I second the motion."

His wife turned on him with a startled look that froze on her face and gave me some idea of what Sodom and Gomorrah must have been like. "You wouldn't," she hissed. "You wouldn't."

"I second Mr. Cullen's motion," said Edward Nash stoutly. "A travelling nude—that's what we need to perfect ourselves as painters."

"You men!" said Mrs. Nash indignantly. "You're all alike. Painters, indeed! Travelling nudes! Mountains and horses are good enough to practice on."

"I'm sure the gentlemen are acting from highest motives," I said, trying to soften things up.

"Lowest motives," cried Mrs. McGregor, "if you ask me."

"Now, now," I said sternly. "Let's have an orderly debate."

"I don't see what there is to debate," said Mrs. Nash. "Lechery. That's all."

In the far corner portly Mr. Barrhead rose. He was about fifty, and he specialized in painting lakes. He was, I believe, a lawyer. "There's some merit in the resolution before us," he began. "However, the whole thing is premature. Our fellow citizens would undoubtedly misconstrue this—this business, and the Community Art Classes would likely get a bad name. In fact, this thing would likely kill the whole development."

"I disagree emphatically, Mr. Chairman," protested Thomas Cullen. "If we get a travelling nude it would be the biggest shot in the arm that painting ever got in this province."

It was at this moment that I saw the travelling nude demurely walk to the hotel in her high-heeled shoes, and I was so engrossed in my vision that I missed most of what followed, though Mrs. Nash threw herself into the battle with renewed vigor and her voice dominated all.

"Question!" someone shouted. "Question!"

"Before we vote," cried Thomas Cullen, obviously trying desperately to save his resolution, "let's ask Mr. Mahler what he thinks."

The noise subsided. All turned to me.

"I think it's an excellent idea," I said firmly. "If there's anything you people need more than anything else it's a travelling nude."

"You can't mean that," cried Mrs. Nash after a moment of stunned silence.

"I do," I said firmly, for my mind was filled with the vision I had seen.

"I knew it," cried Mrs. McGregor. "I knew it all the time."

I have often wondered since what exactly it was that Mrs. McGregor knew.

The vote was taken. Fifty-two against, and one for. Mr. Edward Nash half-raised his hand to vote "aye," but after a quick look at his furious spouse, he dropped it again, and abstained.

IV

It was about two weeks after this memorable scene that my boss in Edmonton summoned me to his office. He's a very nice fellow, though more interested in oil wells than in oil paint, and our relations had always been pleasant enough.

"Ah, Mahler," he greeted me. "It's good to see you. Sit down." He was sucking on a pipe, and began to rummage about for something on his desk. "Everything all right?" he asked casually.

"Fine," I said. "Everything's fine. One more trip to Three Bear Hills and other points South, and that's it for this year. Thank God."

He gave me a quick look. "Why 'Thank God'?" he asked. "Aren't you happy in your work?"

"Oh, sure," I said. "But I'm . . . ."

"Quite so," he interrupted. "Quite so." It was quite obvious that he wasn't really much interested. He was filling his pipe and lighting it, and in between puffs he said, "I called you in, Mahler, because of this," and he held up a letter that he had unearthed from a pile on his desk. "It's nothing," he said nonchalantly. "I'm sure you can explain."

I was getting a bit annoyed, I must admit. If it was nothing, then what was there to explain?

"It's a complaint," he said. "Signed by about fifteen of your students. I think it's a joke or something. But it appears that you are strongly in favor of a travelling nude."

119

I looked him straight in the eye. "That's right," I said. "It's got to the point where you can't have any kind of development of the community art classses unless you get a travelling nude. And the sooner the better." I leaned forward and tapped my knuckles on his desk for emphasis.

"You're not serious," he said.

"I was never more serious in my life," I said. "And what's more, we need the kind of nude that'll really travel in the nude."

"You're not serious," he said again, incredulously. His pipe went out and he sucked on it desperately.

"Furthermore," I continued, quite reckless now, "unless we get a travelling nude, I can't possibly continue to instruct here. I'm sick and tired of mountains and lakes. Our students have to be initiated into the secrets of female, figure, sitting, nude."

"Mahler?" he said, and there was alarm in his voice, "you must be mad."

"Drink deep or taste not the Pierian spring," I said.

"Mahler!" he cried. "What the . . . . "

"The original resolution called for the authorities to secure a travelling nude," I informed him calmly. " 'Authorities' in this case means you. So if I were you, I'd start advertising."

"Mahler," he said. His hands were trembling, and he put his pipe down on his desk. "Please go and see a doctor."

"I will not be insulted," I said haughtily. "I have my artistic pride. It runs in the family. You will have my letter of resignation in the morning."

I left him speechless, poor fellow. I think deep down I must have wanted to give up this job. Don't you?

Oh, I forgot to tell you. The name of the travelling nude was Valerie. She had no surname. Or if she did, I never knew it.

120

Two Sisters
in Geneva

Two Sisters in Geneva

It had been raining all day. Once or twice it had looked as if the rain might let up, and Warren had paid for his coffee and gone out into the street, but the sky was leaden and the rain never stopped at all. That's how it was in Geneva, a waitress told him when he sought refuge again and ordered a glass of beer, once it started to rain like this, it just wouldn't stop for two days and maybe three.

Warren was on his way from Italy to England. He could only stay a day in Geneva and he'd hoped to be able to take a little trip on the Lake, but that was out of the question. In spite of the rain, however, he tried to see as much as he could of the city which John Calvin had made famous, and where the League of Nations had debated in vain. For Warren was studying history at Oxford.

His train left at midnight. By ten o'clock he was tired and wet and worn out and he walked to the station and went into the waiting-room. There were a lot of people there already. The air was damp and steamy-smelling. He sat down beside an old man who was stuffing newspaper into his shoes. The old man said something in French, but Warren couldn't understand him and merely nodded pleasantly, and then pulled a pocket-book

123

out of his over-night bag and started reading. After a while the old man got up with a weary sigh and left, and as he opened the door of the waiting-room two elderly ladies were coming in, followed by a porter carrying their suitcases. The old man held the door open for them, smiling gallantly. The smaller one of the two pushed past him without seeming to notice him, but the other one, who was quite tall and was wearing a broad-brimmed black Italian straw hat, stopped and smiled at him. They exchanged a few words, and then the old man left and closed the door behind him.

"There's room over there," said the smaller of the two ladies. "Over there, Emily."

She walked over and sat down beside Warren. One of the suitcases, Warren noticed, had Canadian Pacific Steamship labels. She took off her felt hat and then her raincoat, and spread her raincoat over one of the suitcases. Then she straightened her beige cardigan and leaned back against the bench. When the other lady joined her, she said, "You should take your hat and coat off, Emily. You're all wet. You don't want to come to England and first thing you know you'll have to go to bed with pneumonia."

"I'm tired," the other one said. "I feel almost as if I had pneumonia already." She talked very slowly and her voice was low and had, thought Warren, a melodious, Italian rhythm. As she talked, she pulled a long pin out of her hair and took the straw hat off. She had black hair, gathered together at the back of her head in a bun. Now that he could see her face plainly, Warren noticed how pale she was.

"I tell you what, Emily. You better go and get something to drink over in the restaurant. Something hot. A cup of tea will do you good. You go and I'll look after the luggage. And then you come back and I'll go. How'll that be?"

"Yes. That will be fine."

"Have you got enough money?"

"Yes. I think so."

"Well, here is some more." She pulled out a purse from

124

her handbag. "Here. This is Swiss money, I think. Yes, it is. All this foreign money!" she exclaimed. "Liras! Francs! It gets a person all confused."

"Ah, well," said the other one. "It's not foreign money to the people who live here." She got up and walked out of the waiting-room.

Warren read a few pages, but he was always conscious of the woman sitting beside him. She fidgeted about on the bench and kept looking over to him, and at last she said, "Oh, you're reading an English book. Then you speak English."

"Yes," said Warren. "I'm a Canadian."

"Are you now, really," she exclaimed. "Well, what a coincidence. I'm from Canada myself. What part of the country do you come from?"

"Toronto," he said.

"How nice," she said. "I live in the West myself. In Edmonton, now. But we used to live up in the North. In the Peace River country. Oh, it's wonderful country, it is. Mr. Miller — that's my husband — he got land up there after the first war, and we homesteaded there. We lived up there for thirty-three years. Until my husband died. Two years ago it is nearly. Well, there wasn't much point me staying there alone. My son and my daughter were gone, so I sold the farm and the car and moved down to the city and got a place not far from my daughter. Thank God Mr. Miller left me well provided for."

"Yes," mumbled Warren. "That's fortunate."

"Oh, he was a good man," said Mrs. Miller. "I met him in England during the war. He was stationed in Yorkshire near where we lived, and we had a real whirlwind romance." She smiled, remembering. "Homesteading sounded very romantic, then. But it wasn't, let me tell you. Irene, my first child, why, she was born during a blizzard in January and you couldn't've got a doctor for love nor money. Even if there'd been one nearby. Which there wasn't. Oh, but Mr. Miller — he wasn't scared. Not much, anyways. He helped right along as if he'd been a midwife all his life. She was born all right. As healthy a baby as you'd ever want to see. Oh, it was backbreaking work, all right, but we made out. Had good years and bad years. It's the good times you really remember, though. And in the end, Mr. Miller left me very well provided for. I think God for that . . . . Stomach. That was always his trouble. It kept getting worse and worse, and finally he died of it."

"I'm sorry," said Warren.

"Isn't that rain awful?" she said. "Still, it's better than that awful heat in Italy. Oh, I couldn't stand that heat. I nearly died of it. I don't know how my sister stood it all these years. I'm trying to persuade her to come and live with me in Canada?"

"Is the other lady your sister?" Warren asked, for he would not have thought it.

"Yes," said Mrs. Miller. "Yes. We don't look much alike, do we? She's the Eyetalian branch of the family." Mrs. Miller gave a little high-pitched laugh. "I'd never have believed that Emily would up and marry an Eyetalian. That was after I'd left for Canada. It must have been — oh — about 1920. My brother Ronald wrote to me and said Emily'd married an Eyetalian and had gone to live in Italy. Well, you could have knocked me down with a feather. Fancy that, I thought. Our Emily an Eyetalian! She'd met him in London, where she'd gone to work after the war. He was a painter, like — an artist. I don't think they ever had much money, and he didn't leave her hardly anything when he died. She's just got enough to live in a furnished room, you know. I was a bit shocked when I saw how she has to live, poor thing. I thought she'd at least have a house. But he didn't leave much. I thank God Mr. Miller left me well provided for. I bought a little house in Edmonton and she'd be most welcome to come and live with me."

"Is she going with you to Canada now?" asked Warren.

"Not just now," said Mrs. Miller. "I only managed to talk her into coming to see the family in England. We've got two sisters and two brothers living in Yorkshire and this'll be the first time in —" she stopped for a moment and calculated silently, "in thirty-six years that we'll all be together. She's

126

never been back in all that time, and neither have I. Only it'd've been easier for her to go back. She had no children and it's not so far. Oh, but I'm sure she'll come and live with me now. There's nothing to keep her in Italy that I can see, and here she'd be with her own flesh and blood. Wouldn't you think it stands to reason?"

"It seems like it," said Warren.

"Where are you coming from now?" asked Mrs. Miller.

"Well, I've just been to Italy, too," he said.

"Oh, have you? Did you go to Florence?"

"Yes," he said, "as a matter of fact, I did."

"Fancy that," said Mrs. Miller. "I might have seen you there. I just spent two weeks there. That's where my sister lives."

"Lovely city," said Warren, but he saw Mrs. Miller shake her head skeptically, and asked, "Didn't you like Florence?"

"Well," she said, "I can't say I really did. Now, mind you, there are some nice things there, all right. I wouldn't deny that. Statues and fountains and churches, like. And my sister took me through some of the museums they have there and I saw some very pretty pictures. But it's all a bit too Papish for me, if you want the truth." She stopped short and looked sharply at Warren. "You're not a Catholic by any chance?"

"No," said Warren, smiling. "Old Presbyterian stock."

"Oh, that's good," she said. "Not that I have anything against Catholics, God forbid. I believe in each person believing as he wants to. But still I must say some of those statues they have — and right out in the open, too — well, I wouldn't have liked it if my daughter had seen them when she was a young girl. And then the heat, too. Oh, it did affect me. But it's a nice enough city otherwise. I'll be glad when I get back to a place where you can understand what people are saying, though. It's a weird feeling hearing people jabbering away and you not understanding a word they're saying."

Neither Warren nor Mrs. Miller noticed her opening the door to the waiting-room, so that she seemed suddenly to be standing there before them.

"Oh, Emily," said Mrs. Miller. "You're back. Did you have some tea?"

"As a matter of fact," she answered, and Warren thought that her eyes glinted ironically, "I had some brandy. It's better than tea."

"Oh, well," said Mrs. Miller tolerantly. "Once in a while it's all right. That's what my husband used to say. But he never held with drinking. Oh, Emily. There's a young Canadian gentleman here. Mr. —"

"Douglas," he said. "Warren Douglas."

"Mr. Douglas. And that's my sister. Mrs. Emily Bun — . . . Bun —. . . Oh, I never can remember how to pronounce that name."

"Buonarroti. Emilia Buonarroti."

"Well, I never can get over it," said Mrs. Miller. "It never does sound like our Emily."

Mrs. Buonarroti sat down and, turning to Warren, she said quietly, "Buonarroti was the family name of the great Michelangelo. My husband belonged to a branch of the same family." She had taken off her coat, and Warren saw that she was wearing a black silk dress which looked very old-fashioned.

"I think I'll go off and have a cup of tea myself," said Mrs. Miller. "If you'll excuse me."

Warren watched her walk out of the waiting-room. Her shoes were sturdy and new, and she wore a good worsted skirt and a beige cardigan over a frilly white blouse.

"You are a student?" said Mrs. Buonarroti.

"Yes," said Warren. "How did you know?"

"My husband taught for many years. The history of Renaissance art — that was his subject. So I knew many students. All students look alike," she said and smiled at him.

"That's very interesting," he said. "Your husband being a scholar, I mean. I thought he was a painter. I mean, that's what your sister said."

128

"Oh, yes, he painted, too," she said. "But he was not a professional painter. He was a good painter, but not a professional painter." She sat there thinking for a while, and then she said, "My husband was a very interesting man. And to live with him was, yes, a great privilege. You know, Mr. Douglas, I was an ignorant girl when I married, and my husband taught me such a lot. Of course, when you live in Firenze — in Florence — you have to learn something. Art, religion, history — it is all preserved around you."

"I am reading history now at Oxford," Warren said.

"But my sister said you are from Canada."

"I am, but I am studying at Oxford."

"It is strange speaking English again after so many years. I hardly talked English at all for years and years, and when my sister came, I could hardly speak it any more. I had to practice first." She laughed. "My husband could speak English, but after the first year or two we always talked in Italian . . . . He was a wonderful man — my husband. But the war — it was too much for him. He was never too strong, and it was hard to get enough coal. It was too much for him. He died only a few weeks before the end of the war." She began to cough, at first lightly, and then more violently, until her whole body trembled and Warren was quite concerned.

"Is there — is there anything I can get you?" he stammered, not knowing what to do.

She shook her head and gradually she stopped coughing. "I'm sorry," she said. "It's this terrible rain and this dampness. I can't stand all this wet. As soon as we left Italy I began to feel it, you know. Perhaps I was only imagining things at first, but as soon as we came to Geneva it was very real. I hate rain and dull, cloudy skies. And this is all just a foretaste of what it will be like in England. Gray skies and rain and rain and rain." She shuddered. "And what will I say to them all when I am in England? To my brothers and sisters?" She seemed for a moment to be talking to herself alone, for she dropped her voice and her eyes looked across the waiting-room in the

129

direction of the station restaurant where Mrs. Miller would now be drinking her tea.

She turned again to Warren. "We have been living in different worlds," she said. "Much too different. My sister is such a good woman. So kind and so well-meaning. But after two days, Mr. Douglas — well, we didn't have anything to say to each other. She told me about how they built their farm, and about blizzards, and how her children were born, and how they became well off, and I — well, I tried to show her Florence, and I'll never forget how shocked she was when I took her to the Piazza della Signoria and she saw in the Loggia statues of nude figures — famous works by Cellini and Giambologna. It was quite funny, really, but also sad. And it will be the same thing when I meet the others. It will rain and we will all be crowded together in a room and I will long to go back home to Italy. I wish now I was waiting for a train to take me back to Florence. . . . Do you know Italy, Mr. Douglas?"

"A little," he said. "I've just been in Florence and Venice. I loved them both, but especially Venice."

Mrs. Buonarroti turned her pale face to him and looked musingly at him. "Yes," she said. "Yes. At first it is always Venice. In Venice everything is out in the open, and you — you are so — so — well . . . ."

"Overwhelmed." Warren supplied the word.

"Yes," said Mrs. Buonarroti. "Overwhelmed. Your eyes cannot take it all in at once. But Florence opens herself only slowly, until you see her full beauty. My husband didn't like Venice. Not enough secrets, he said. Of course, he was a Florentine, and that explains a lot. But really there is nothing in the world that is so beautiful as to look down at Florence from Fiesole just when the sun goes down, and to see the hills and the mountains and the cypress trees and the wonderful city in the plain. Nothing."

"You will miss all this," said Warren, "if you go to Canada."

She looked at him quickly. "To Canada? Why should I go

130

to Canada?"

"Oh, but Mrs. Miller — your sister . . . ."

Mrs. Buonarroti shrugged her shoulders and smiled. "My sister is such a kind person," she said, "but she doesn't understand. From the room where I live I can look out and see the wonderful campanile, and I can walk along the Arno, and once a week I take a bus to Fiesole. Florence is my city, Mr. Douglas . . . . I don't know whether you understand."

"I think I do," said Warren.

"To live in a strange land in a strange city with my sister would be — well not exactly like the Inferno, but like Purgatorio."

They both laughed.

A minute or two afterwards Mrs. Miller returned.

"Well," she said, "that was nice and hot. Mind you, they don't know how to make a cup of tea here. Or in Italy. The water's never boiling when they pour it. That's the trouble." She turned to her sister. "Well, I hope the young gentleman's been telling you all about Canada."

"I'm afraid Mrs. Buonarroti has been telling me about Italy," said Warren.

"I knew it," said Mrs. Miller. "Emily does love talking about Italy. Oh, well. You just wait till you see the wide-open prairie, Emily, and the Rocky Mountains. Once you live there, you'll never again want to live anywhere else. I know I wouldn't. Why, I couldn't live in England again, let alone in Italy. Everything's all crammed together so."

Just then Mrs. Buonarroti began to cough again and she had to get up to catch her breath. Warren and Mrs. Miller both jumped up and supported her, and after a while the fit subsided and she sat down on the bench, exhausted.

"The dry climate out West will do her the world of good," said Mrs. Miller to Warren. "It will clear this up in no time."

Over the public address system there came an announcement. The express to Paris and Calais was arriving.

131

"That's our train," said Warren. "Should I go and get a porter?"

Mrs. Miller nodded.

When he returned with the porter, the ladies put on their coats and hats. Mrs. Buonarroti took hold of Warren's arm and they walked out onto the platform. The rain was still coming down in steady, thin strings.

"How I hate this rain," said Mrs. Buonarroti, speaking very softly, "and how I wish I was back in Florence."

The Broken Globe

The Broken Globe

Since it was Nick Solchuk who first told me about the
opening in my field at the University of Alberta, I went up to see
him as soon as I received word that I had been appointed. He
lived in one of those old mansions in Pimlico that had once
served as town houses for wealthy merchants and aristocrats,
but now housed a less moneyed group of people —
stenographers, students, and intellectuals of various kinds. He
had studied at Cambridge and got his doctorate there and was
now doing research at the Imperial College and rapidly
establishing a reputation among the younger men for his work
on problems which had to do with the curvature of the earth.

His room was on the third floor, and it was very cramped,
but he refused to move because he could look out from his
window and see the Thames and the steady flow of boats, and
that gave him a sense of distance and of space also. Space, he
said, was what he missed most in the crowded city. He referred
to himself, nostalgically, as a prairie boy, and when he wanted
to demonstrate what he meant by space he used to say that
when a man stood and looked out across the open prairie, it
was possible for him to believe that the earth was flat.

"So," he said, after I had told him my news, "you are

going to teach French to prairie boys and girls. I congratulate you." Then he cocked his head to one side, and looked me over and said: "How are your ears?"

"My ears?" I said. "They're all right. Why?"

"Prepare yourself," he said. "Prairie voices trying to speak French — that will be a great experience for you. I speak from experience. I learned my French pronunciation in a little one-room school in a prairie village. From an extraordinary girl, mind you, but her mind ran to science. Joan McKenzie — that was her name. A wiry little thing, sharp-nosed, and she always wore brown dresses. She was particularly fascinated by earthquakes. 'In 1755 the city of Lisbon, Portugal, was devastated. Sixty-thousand persons died; the shock was felt in Southern France and North Africa; and inland waters of Great Britain and Scandinavia were agitated.' You see, I still remember that, and I can hear her voice too. Listen: 'In common with the entire solar system, the earth is moving through space at the rate of approximately 45,000 miles per hour, toward the constellation of Hercules. Think of that, boys and girls.' Well, I thought about it. It was a lot to think about. Maybe that's why I became a geophysicist. Her enthusiasm was infectious. I knew her at her peak. After a while she got tired and married a solid farmer and had eight children."

"But her French, I take it, was not so good," I said.

"No," he said. "Language gave no scope to her imagination. Mind you, I took French seriously enough. I was a very serious student. For a while I even practiced French pronunciation at home. But I stopped it because it bothered my father. My mother begged me to stop. For the sake of peace."

"Your father's ears were offended," I said.

"Oh, no," Nick said, "not his ears. His soul. He was sure that I was learning French so I could run off and marry a French girl . . . . Don't laugh. It's true. When once my father believed something, it was very hard to shake him."

"But why should he have objected to your marrying a

136

French girl anyway?"

"Because," said Nick, and pointed a stern finger at me, "because when he came to Canada he sailed from some French port, and he was robbed of all his money while he slept. He held all Frenchmen responsible. He never forgot and he never forgave. And, by God, he wasn't going to have that cursed language spoken in his house. He wasn't going to have any nonsense about science talked in his house either." Nick was silent for a moment, and then he said, speaking very quietly, "Curious man, my father. He had strange ideas, but a strange kind of imagination, too. I couldn't understand him when I was going to school or to the university. But then a year or two ago, I suddenly realized that the shape of the world he lived in had been forever fixed for him by some medieval priest in the small Ukrainian village where he was born and where he received an education of sorts when he was a boy. And I suddenly realized that he wasn't mad, but that he lived in the universe of the medieval church. The earth for him was the centre of the universe, and the centre was still. It didn't move. The sun rose in the East and it set in the West, and it moved perpetually around a still earth. God had made this earth especially for man, and man's function was to perpetuate himself and to worship God. My father never said all that in so many words, mind you, but that is what he believed. Everything else was heresy."

He fell silent.

"How extraordinary," I said.

He did not answer at once, and after a while he said, in a tone of voice which seemed to indicate that he did not want to pursue the matter further, "Well, when you are in the middle of the Canadian West, I'll be in Rome. I've been asked to give a paper to the International Congress of Geophysicists which meets there in October."

"So I heard," I said. "Wilcocks told me the other day. He said it was going to be a paper of some importance. In fact, he said it would create a stir."

"Did Wilcocks really say that?" he asked eagerly, his face

137

reddening, and he seemed very pleased. We talked for a while longer, and then I rose to go.

He saw me to the door and was about to open it for me, but stopped suddenly, as if he were turning something over in his mind, and then said quickly, "Tell me — would you do something for me?"

"Of course," I said. "If I can."

He motioned me back to my chair and I sat down again. "When you are in Alberta," he said, "and if it is convenient for you, would you — would you go to see my father?"

"Why, yes," I stammered, "why, of course. I — I didn't realize he was still . . . ."

"Oh, yes," he said, "he's still alive, still working. He lives on his farm, in a place called Three Bear Hills, about sixty or seventy miles out of Edmonton. He lives alone. My mother is dead. I have a sister who is married and lives in Calgary. There were only the two of us. My mother could have no more children. It was a source of great agony for them. My sister goes to see him sometimes, and then she sometimes writes to me. He never writes to me. We — we had — what shall I call it — differences. If you went to see him and told him that I had not gone to the devil, perhaps . . . " He broke off abruptly, clearly agitated, and walked over to his window and stood staring out, then said, "Perhaps you'd better not. I — I don't want to impose on you."

I protested that he was not imposing at all, and promised that I would write to him as soon as I had paid my visit.

I met him several times after that, but he never mentioned the matter again.

I sailed from England about the middle of August and arrived in Montreal a week later. The long journey West was one of the most memorable experiences I have ever had. There were moments of weariness and dullness. But the very monotony was impressive. There was a grandeur about it. It was monotony of a really monumental kind. There were moments when, exhausted by the sheer impact of the landscape, I thought back with longing to the tidy, highly cultivated countryside of England and of France, to the sight of men and women working in the fields, to the steady succession of villages and towns, and everywhere the consciousness of nature humanized. But I also began to understand why Nick Solchuk was always longing for more space and more air, especially when we moved into the prairies, and the land became flatter until there seemed nothing, neither hill nor tree nor bush, to disturb the vast unbroken flow of land until in the far distance a thin, blue line marked the point where the prairie merged into the sky. Yet over all there was a strange tranquillity, all motion seemed suspended, and only the sun moved steadily, imperturbably West, dropping finally over the rim of the horizon, a blazing red ball, but leaving a superb evening light lying over the land still.

I was reminded of the promise I had made, but when I arrived in Edmonton, the task of settling down absorbed my time and energy so completely that I did nothing about it. Then, about the middle of October, I saw a brief report in the newspaper about the geophysical congress which had opened in Rome on the previous day, and I was mindful of my promise again. Before I could safely bury it in the back of my mind again, I sat down and wrote a brief letter to Nick's father, asking him when I could come out to visit him. Two weeks passed without an answer, and I decided to go and see him on the next Saturday without further formalities.

The day broke clear and fine. A few white clouds were in the metallic autumn sky and the sun shone coldly down upon the earth, as if from a great distance. I drove south as far as Wetaskiwin and then turned east. The paved highway gave way to gravel and got steadily worse. I was beginning to wonder whether I was going right, when I rounded a bend and a grain elevator hove like a signpost into view. It was now about three o'clock and I had arrived in Three Bear Hills, but, as Nick had told me, there were neither bears nor hills here, but only prairie, and suddenly the beginning of an embryonic street with a few buildings on either side like a small island in a vast sea, and then all was prairie again.

I stopped in front of the small general store and went in to ask for directions. Three farmers were talking to the storekeeper, a bald, bespectacled little man who wore a long, dirty apron, and stood leaning against his counter. They stopped talking and turned to look at me. I asked where the Solchuk farm was.

Slowly scrutinizing me, the storekeeper asked, "You just new here?"

"Yes," I said.

"From the old country, eh?"

"Yes."

"You selling something?"

"No, no," I said. "I — I teach at the University."

"That so?" He turned to the other men and said, "Only boy ever went to University from around here was Solchuk's boy, Nick. Real brainy young kid, Nick. Two of 'em never got on together. Too different. You know."

They nodded slowly.

"But that boy of his — he's a real big-shot scientist now. You know them addem bombs and them hydrergen bombs. He helps make 'em."

"No, no," I broke in quickly. "That's not what he does. He's a geophysicist."

"What's that?" asked one of the men.

But before I could answer, the little storekeeper asked excitedly, "You know Nick?"

"Yes," I said, "we're friends. I've come to see his father."

"And where's he now? Nick, I mean."

"Right now he is in Rome," I said. "But he lives in London, and does research there."

"Big-shot, eh," said one of the men laconically, but with a trace of admiration in his voice, too.

"He's a big scientist, though, like I said. Isn't that so?" the storekeeper broke in.

140

"He's going to be a very important scientist indeed," I said, a trifle solemnly.

"Like I said," he called out triumphantly. "That's showing 'em. A kid from Three Bear Hills, Alberta. More power to him!" His pride was unmistakable. "Tell me, mister," he went on, his voice dropping, "does he remember this place sometimes? Or don't he want to know us no more?"

"Oh no," I said quickly. "He often talks of this place, and of Alberta, and of Canada. Some day he plans to return."

"That's right," he said with satisfaction. He drew himself up to full height, banged his fist on the table and said, "I'm proud of that boy. Maybe old Solchuk don't think so much of him, but you tell him old Mister Marshall is proud of him." He came from behind the counter and almost ceremoniously escorted me out to my car and showed me the way to Solchuk's farm.

I had about another five miles to drive, and the road, hardly more now than two black furrows cut into the prairie, was uneven and bumpy. The land was fenced on both sides of the road, and at last I came to a rough wooden gate hanging loosely on one hinge, and beyond it there was a cluster of small wooden buildings. The largest of these, the house itself, seemed at one time to have been ochre-colored, but the paint had worn off and it now looked curiously mottled. A few chickens were wandering about, pecking at the ground, and from the back I could hear the grunting and squealing of pigs.

I walked up to the house and, just as I was about to knock, the door was suddenly opened, and a tall, massively built old man stood before me.

"My name is . . . " I began.

But he interrupted me. "You the man wrote to me?" His voice, though unpolished, had the same deep timbre as Nick's.

"That's right," I said.

"You a friend of Nick?"

"Yes."

He beckoned me in with a nod of his head. The door was

low and I had to stoop a bit to get into the room. It was a large, low-ceilinged room. A smallish window let in a patch of light which lit up the middle of the room but did not spread into the corners, so that it seemed as if it were perpetually dusk. A table occupied the centre, and on the far side there was a large wood stove on which stood a softly hissing black kettle. In the corner facing the entrance there was an iron bedstead, and the bed was roughly made, with a patchwork quilt thrown carelessly on top.

The old man gestured me to one of the chairs which stood around the table.

"Sit."

I did as he told me, and he sat down opposite me and placed his large calloused hands before him on the table. He seemed to study me intently for a while, and I scrutinized him. His face was covered by a three-day's stubble, but in spite of that, and in spite of the fact that it was a face beaten by sun and wind, it was clear that he was Nick's father. For Nick had the same determined mouth, and the same high cheekbones and the same dark, penetrating eyes.

At last he spoke. "You friend of Nick."

I nodded my head.

"What he do now?" he asked sharply. "He still tampering with the earth?"

His voice rose as if he were delivering a challenge, and I drew back involuntarily. "Why — he's doing scientific research, yes," I told him. "He's . . ."

"What God has made," he said sternly, "no man should touch."

Before I could regain my composure, he went on, "He sent you. What for? What he want?"

"Nothing," I said, "nothing at all. He sent me to bring you greetings and to tell you he is well."

"And you come all the way from Edmonton to tell me?"

"Yes, of course."

A faint smile played about his mouth, and the features of his face softened. Then suddenly he rose from his chair and

142

stood towering over me. "You are welcome in this house," he said.

The formality with which he spoke was quite extraordinary and seemed to call for an appropriate reply, but I could do little more than stammer a thank you, and he, assuming again a normal tone of voice, asked me if I cared to have coffee. When I assented he walked to the far end of the room and busied himself about the stove.

It was then that I noticed, just under the window, a rough little wooden table and on top of it a faded old globe made of cardboard, such as little children use in school. I was intrigued to see it there and went over to look at it more closely. The cheap metal mount was brown with rust, and when I lifted it and tried to turn to globe on its axis, I found that it would not rotate because part of it had been squashed and broken. I ran my hand over the deep dent, and suddenly the old man startled me.

"What you doing there?" Curiosity seemed mingled with suspicion in his voice and made me feel like a small child surprised by its mother in an unauthorized raid on the pantry. I set down the globe and turned. He was standing by the table with two big mugs of coffee in his hands.

"Coffee is hot," he said.

I went back to my chair and sat down, slightly embarrassed.

"Drink," he said, pushing one of the mugs over to me.

We both began to sip the coffee, and for some time neither of us said anything.

"That thing over there," he said at last, putting down his mug, "that thing you was looking at — he brought it home one day — he was a boy then — maybe thirteen-year-old — Nick. The other day I found it up in the attic. I was going to throw it in the garbage. But I forgot. There it belongs. In the garbage. It is a false thing." His voice had now become venomous.

"False?" I said. "How is it false?"

143

He disregarded my question. "I remember," he went on, "he came home from school one day and we was all here in this room — all sitting around this table eating supper, his mother, his sister and me and Alex, too — the hired man like. And then sudden-like Nick pipes up, and he says, we learned in school today, he says, how the earth is round like a ball, he says, and how it moves around and around the sun and never stops, he says. They learning you rubbish in school, I say. But he says no, Miss McKenzie never told him no lies. Then I say she does, I say, and a son of mine shouldn't believe it. Stop your ears! Let not Satan come in!" He raised an outspread hand and his voice thundered as if he were a prophet armed. "But he was always a stubborn boy — Nick. Like a mule. He never listened to reason. I believe it, he says. To me he says that — his father, just like that. I believe it, he says, because science has proved it and it is the truth. It is false, I cry, and you will not believe it. I believe it, he says. So then I hit him because he will not listen and will not obey. But he keeps shouting and shouting and shouting. She moves, he shouts, she moves, she moves!"

He stopped. His hands had balled themselves into fists, and the remembered fury sent the blood streaming into his face. He seemed now to have forgotten my presence and he went on speaking in a low murmuring voice, almost as if he were telling the story to himself.

"So the next day, or the day after, I go down to that school, and there is this little Miss McKenzie, so small and so thin that I could have crush her with my bare hands. What you teaching my boy Nick? I ask her. What false lies you stuffing in his head? What you telling him that the earth is round and that she moves for? Did Joshua tell the earth to stand still, or did he command the sun? So she says to me, I don't care what Joshua done, she says, I will tell him what science has discovered. With that woman I could get nowhere. So then I try to keep him away from school, and I lock him up in the house, but it was not good. He got out, and he run to the school like, and Miss McKenzie she sends me a letter to say she will send up the inspectors if I try to keep him away from the school. And I could do nothing."

His sense of impotence was palpable. He sat sunk into himself as if he were still contemplating ways of halting the scientific education of his son.

"Two, three weeks after," he went on, "he comes walking in this door with a large paper parcel in his hand. Now, he calls out to me, now I will prove it to you, I will prove that she moves. And he tears off the paper from the box and takes out this — this thing, and he puts it on the table here. Here, he cries, here is the earth, and look, she moves. And he gives that thing a little push and it twirls around like. I have to laugh. A toy, I say to him, you bring me a toy here, not bigger than my hand, and it is supposed to be the world, this little toy here, with the printed words on colored paper, this little cardboard ball. This Miss McKenzie, I say to him, she's turning you crazy in that school. But look, he says, she moves. Now I have to stop my laughing. I'll soon show you she moves, I say, for he is beginning to get me mad again. And I go up to the table and I take the toy thing in my hands and I smash it down like this."

He raised his fists and let them crash down on the table as if he meant to splinter it.

"That'll learn you, I cry. I don't think he could believe I had done it, because he picks up the thing and he tries to turn it, but it don't turn no more. He stands there and the tears roll down his cheeks, and then, sudden-like, he takes the thing in both his hands and he throws it at me. And it would have hit me right in the face, for sure, if I did not put up my hand. Against your father, I cry, you will raise up your hand against your father. Asmodeus! I grab him by the arm, and I shake him and I beat him like he was the devil. And he makes me madder and madder because he don't cry or shout or anything. And I would have kill him there, for sure, if his mother didn't come in then and pull me away. His nose was bleeding, but he didn't notice. Only he looks at me and says, you can beat me and break my globe, but you can't stop her moving. That night my wife she make me swear by all that's holy that I wouldn't touch him no more. And from then on I never hit him again nor talk to him about this thing. He goes his way and I go mine."

He fell silent. Then after a moment he snapped suddenly, "You hold with that?"

"Hold with what?" I asked, taken aback.

"With that thing?" He pointed behind him at the little table and at the broken globe. His gnarled hands now tightly interlocked, he leaned forward in his chair and his dark, brooding eyes sought an answer from mine in the twilight of the room.

Alone with him there, I was almost afraid to answer firmly. Was it because I feared that I would hurt him too deeply if I did, or was I perhaps afraid that he would use violence on me as he had on Nick?

I cleared my throat. "Yes," I said then. "Yes, I believe that the earth is round and that she moves. That fact has been accepted now for a long time."

I expected him to round on me but he seemed suddently to have grown very tired, and in a low resigned voice he said, "Satan has taken over all the world." Then suddenly he roused himself and hit the table hard with his fist, and cried passionately, "But not me! Not me!"

It was unbearable. I felt that I must break the tension, and I said the first thing that came into my mind. "You can be proud of your son in spite of all that happened between you. He is a fine man, and the world honors him for his work."

He gave me a long look, "He should have stayed here," he said quietly. "When I die, there will be nobody to look after the land. Instead he has gone off to tamper with God's earth."

His fury was now all spent. We sat for a while in silence, and then I rose. Together we walked out of the house. When I was about to get into my car, he touched me lightly on the arm. I turned. His eyes surveyed the vast expanse of sky and land, stretching far into the distance, reddish clouds in the sky and blue shadows on the land. With a gesture of great dignity and power he lifted his arm and stood pointing into the distance, at the flat land and the low-hanging sky. "Look," he said, very slowly and very quietly, "she is flat, and she stands still."

It was impossible not to feel a kind of admiration for the old man. There was something heroic about him. I held out my hand and he took it. He looked at me steadily, then averted his eyes and said, "Send greetings to my son."

I drove off quickly, but had to stop again in order to open the wooden gate. I looked back at the house, and saw him still standing there, still looking at his beloved land, a lonely, towering figure framed against the darkening evening sky.

Credits:

Editor: R. Silvester
Publisher: J. Lewis
Cover and Title Pages: Norman Yates
Typesetting: Mary Albert
Layout: Mike Wiebe
Printing and Binding: Co-op Press Ltd., Edmonton and Universal
Book Bindery, Edmonton
Financial Assistance:
        Alberta Culture,
        Canada Council,
        Multiculturalism Program, Government of Canada,
        Nova: An Alberta Corporation.